THE LAST TIGER

THE LAST TIGER

MY FAVOURITE ANIMAL STORIES

RUSKIN BOND

ALEPH

ALEPH BOOK COMPANY
An independent publishing firm
promoted by *Rupa Publications India*

First published in India in 2023
by Aleph Book Company
7/16 Ansari Road, Daryaganj
New Delhi 110 002

ISBN: 978-93-93852-54-0

1 3 5 7 9 10 8 6 4 2

Printed in India.

CONTENTS

INTRODUCTION
THE STORY OF THE STORIES

'How can there be an India without tigers?'

This was the last line of my story, first published by Khushwant Singh in the *Illustrated Weekly of India* back in the late 1960s. It was a time when the number of tigers in the country had fallen to an alarming low, and there were fears that it might even become extinct in a few years' time. Fortunately, thanks to vigorous campaigns by enlightened citizens and environmentalists, the magnificent animal survived the lean years and is with us today, alive and well, and still the king of the forest and symbolic of a resurgent India.

My story was relevant at the time it was published, and it is relevant today, because our wildlife continues to be at risk, due to relentless urbanization and the shrinking of our green cover. While we preserve our tigers, we must also take care of the birds, animals, and small creatures that are in danger of disappearing. How can there be an India without beautiful parrots, pheasants, kingfishers, cormorants, and flamingoes? Even the wily crow is part of our heritage, and I don't see so many of them around today.

∽

Leopards, on the other hand, appear to be on the increase, and have even become a menace to the people living in remote villages in Garhwal and Kumaon. There are even instances of villages being abandoned because of the depredations of these bold and clever animals. My story 'Panther's Moon' was written some years ago, but it's a true story and reflects the dilemma that many hill folk face today.

∽

I must tell you an amusing story about 'The Last Tiger'. Shortly after it was first published, a film producer bought the film rights from me for a modest sum of five thousand rupees. (Not bad fifty years ago!) The late Tom Alter acted in it, as one of the shikaris. He told me that they hired a tiger from a local circus, but that the tiger was very temperamental and was always trying to get back to its cage, in anticipation of a regular meal—lunch and dinner at fixed times—why bother to chase fleet-footed gazelles? However, the film was completed, but no one saw it, because no distributor would take it up and it never found its way to the screen, big or small. They called the film *Tiger Uncle*. No wonder it was doomed.

∽

Over the years I have written a number of stories about Grandfather and his odd assortments of pets, ranging from tiger cubs to chameleons and cassowary birds. Of course he didn't keep all of them at the same time, that would have driven my poor grandmother crazy. I was just an infant when he died, so most of the happenings were recounted by my mother, and I turned them into magazine stories and children's books, which were published here and in other countries. Some of them are perennial favourites and keep popping up in anthologies and school readers.

I should mention that the grandfather in 'The Regimental Myna' was my paternal grandfather. He was a foot soldier in Kipling's time, constantly route-marching across the country. He did get to see a lot of India because he was married in Jubbalpur, and had three sons who were born respectively in Barrackpore, Shahjahanpur (my father), and Chittagong. We are all part of India's history.

But Private Bond did not get time for keeping pets, apart from the hardy and cheeky myna who followed him everywhere.

Back in the 1970s, a comical case was brought against me for an allegedly 'obscene' story that was published in a Bombay magazine, and I had to travel to Bombay to appear in court. I took the slow passenger train from Dehradun, a journey that lasted two days and two nights, the train stopping at every small station as it took its time chugging along through field, forest, and desert. It was at Raiwala, Haridwar, that a myna flew into my compartment (shared with three other travellers), keeping us company for a day and a night, seemingly quite at home, as if it was in the habit of undertaking long railway journeys. This sociable bird only left us at a small station in Rajasthan, when it flew out of an open window into the vastness of the desert state. I worried about that bird. Would it evet get back to Raiwala, to home and family? But mynas are good survivors. It would probably settle down at a railway station. It was a railway bird, after all. Perhaps it would take the next train back to Dehradun.

Anyway, that little bird brought me luck (as its ancestors did for my grandfather), and the case went my way, and I went on to write many more stories—having learnt that it's safer to write about birds and beasts than it is to write about the human animal.

New to this collection is my reminiscence of the little mountain stream that played an important part in my life when I first came to live in the hills. A fox, a leopard (or panther, if you prefer), and various birds and beetles helped a small-town writer discover the never-ending story of the world of nature.

Ruskin Bond

September 2022

THE CALL OF THE LEOPARD

'Unneow, unneow', came the monotonous call of the barbet, from the topmost branches of a deodar. 'Injustice, injustice!' is the English translation of its call. The barbet is said to be a reincarnation of a moneylender who died before he could recover all his dues. Sufficient reason to complain.

I could hear the barbet from my cottage, Maplewood, where I spent the first ten years of my sojourn in these hills. It was summertime, and I could hear it whenever I happened to be rambling. The cottage was near the forest, and I have described it in 'Song of the Forest'. Some of the forest dwellers who visited me are described in 'Guests Who Come in from the Forest'. But it was only when I discovered the stream at the bottom of the hill that I became fully aware of all that my natural surroundings had to offer by way of birds, beasts, and green growing things.

It was a shallow stream, running over a rocky bed, and I could roll up my trousers and wade in it, disturbing the tadpoles and minnows who fled to the shelter of little inlets. Also wading, at some distance from me, was a spotted forktail, an elegant bird, who hopped from rock to rock rather like Fred Astaire, that wonderful dancer in the old musicals. There were long-tailed magpies, a noisy lot, and a woodpecker hard at work, trying to extract a small beetle from its fortress in the trunk of an old oak tree. Don't woodpeckers ever get tired? This woodpecker would be knocking away for hours. Knock, knock, knock on wood!

Oh, I must tell you about the fox.

You don't see many foxes in these parts, but one of the first wild creatures that I encountered was this beautiful, bushy-tailed fox. It was late evening, and I was walking home from the town when I saw this fox dancing in the middle of the footpath. Later, I wrote a poem about it. I don't write many poems, but this one just happened, and I called it 'Lone Fox Dancing':

As I walked home last night
I saw a lone fox dancing
In the bright moonlight.

I stood and watched,
Then took the low road, knowing
The night was his by right.

Sometimes when words ring true,
I'm like a lone fox dancing
In the morning dew.

I was to see that little fox quite often. Unlike me, he wasn't into poetry, but intent on making forays into Major Powell's poultry farm higher up the hill. Major Powell lost a lot of birds to that fox, and to various wild cats, and he lost money on his enterprise. 'A fowl subject,' he would grumble. 'I should have stuck to growing mushrooms.'

In his younger days he had been a shikari, a hunter, and had shot a number of tigers and leopards, all man-eaters, or so he claimed. The population of man-eating tigers must have been enormous, judging by the frequence of their mortality. Anyway, I must tell you about the major's invention, a contraption that was supposed to replicate the mating call of a leopard.

He put together a wooden box—about the size of a hat box—and pierced a hole in its side. Into this hole he inserted a coil of metal wire. When you drew the wire back and forth it made a sound very similar to the 'sawing' of a leopard on the prowl—presumably in search of a mate.

'Let's try it out,' said the major enthusiastically, and led me to a grassy knoll above the stream. It was late evening, the sun was just going down. Major Powell began working the wire, to and fro. The sound it produced was quite eerie.

We took turns working on the box but we heard no responsive call. The 'Indian Love Call', to be effective, must be sung as a duet. But the forest was silent.

We were about to give up when we heard a grunt from behind, and looking up, we saw a beautiful leopard perched on a flat rock about fifty feet above us. He (or was it a she?) was watching us with some interest, obviously puzzled by the strange sound we were making.

Major Powell swung round with his gun (almost knocking me over) and fired it at the beast, missing it by some distance. The leopard took off, vanishing into the woods.

'Perverted brute,' complained the major. 'Coming at us from behind!'

'Corbett wouldn't have missed,' I remarked, after which he refused to talk to me for a week. But I had to admit that his invention had, indeed, summoned up the leopard.

∽

I felt safer exploring the stream without the presence of Major Powell.

A leopard had been active in the vicinity. I found the partially eaten carcass of a cow on the banks of the stream. The small hill cows are easy prey for a leopard. The barking deer or kakar, its natural prey, was quite abundant in the surrounding hills; but it is always on the alert, very sensitive to the presence of danger, and it is swift in flight. A lazy leopard would just as soon seize a domestic animal; a goat or a dog makes a good dinner.

On my exploration of the stream I came across someone who wasn't bothered by leopards, jackals, snakes, or other forest dwellers.

Walking upstream for about half a mile, I found a small clearing and a covered platform which turned out to be a cremation ground used by local villagers and the poorer residents of the hill station. (The more affluent were taken to Haridwar for their last rites.) Beside this platform was a small hut occupied by a caretaker, who lived there night and day, keeping a watchful eye on a large pile of firewood that he had gathered from the forest in anticipation of an occasional cremation.

He was a small man, not very communicative but quite friendly. He was used to living alone for long periods, and the nature of his work couldn't be described as cheerful or exhilarating, but he had three lively companions—three terrier-like dogs, very similar to each other, and all three decked out in colourful jackets. One had a green jacket, one an orange jacket, and the third a purple jacket. These were designed to protect the dogs from the cold—down there in the shadowed ravine, winter nights could be very cold—and this strange man had stitched them himself. Each dog also wore a collar studded with steel spikes. The collars were meant to protect them from marauding leopards, for a leopard will usually seize its victim by the neck and then fling it into the air (if it's a small animal), breaking its neck in the process. These collars must have been effective, because the caretaker hadn't lost any dogs. A wily leopard wouldn't care to have its jaws full of sharp steel impediments.

The caretaker always had a fire going, and he cooked for himself and his dogs. He was paid something by the municipality. But the spot was so hard to reach—a steep descent from the town—that cremations were now few, most people preferring to take the road to Rajpur and Dehradun.

During my years in Maplewood I would see them quite often. The silent man in search of firewood, the silent dogs in their colourful jackets following him everywhere. The dogs were silent too, I never heard them barking.

After I'd left Maplewood and moved further up the hill, I heard that this little cremation ground had been abandoned. I wondered what had happened to the caretaker and his dogs. I never saw them again but they appeared to be good survivors.

∽

A silent place the hillside, except for the sound of rushing water—and that barbet! Would he ever recover his money?

Naturally, I preferred walking downstream. As the hill grew steeper, the stream grew bigger, collecting the waters of springs and tributaries. Small pools were formed. There were waterfalls. Clumps of ferns sprang up on the banks. I was followed downstream by the langurs— those handsome, long-tailed simians, leaping gracefully from tree to tree; and by the inquisitive forktail, hopping elegantly from rock to rock.

It was all downhill, and I was far from elegant, stumbling amongst the jagged rocks and moss-covered boulders. No Spiderman, I had to give up and retreat to calmer waters.

The stream rushed on, of course—down to the valley to join the little Song River, and the Song would join the gentle Suswa, and together they would wander about the wide valley, picking up friends and followers, flowing into the Ganga above Haridwar, and then continuing their long journey as one great river across the wide flat plains, to become part of the Indian Ocean. And my little stream was an accessory to this great adventure.

All this is memory, of course. I am now far too old to be scrambling up steep hillsides or negotiating boulder-strewn streams. But I keep my good memories stowed away in my mind—my 'thinking heart'—and I return to them from time to time, as one returns to memories of old friends and far-off times and faraway places.

SONG OF THE FOREST

We think of forests as places of solitude and silence, except when tigers roar and elephants trumpet; but there are always sounds, more subtle than these, that come to the notice of the sensitive wanderer.

Many years ago I lived in a small cottage on the edge of the forest, on the outskirts of the hill station of Mussoorie. A steep and narrow footpath led down through oaks and maples to the red-roofed house that was to be my home for several years.

It was early summer, and when I opened the windows I was assailed by the strident chorus of hundreds of cicadas informing me, and anyone who cared to listen, that it would be raining before long. The cicadas make their shrill music by scraping their legs against their quivering bodies. It's hard to find them—they merge with the trunks of the trees they inhabit—but they are there all summer, constantly reminding you of their presence.

I was a great walker in those days, and my walks took me down to the stream at the bottom of the hill. It made its own sounds, as it tumbled over the rocks and pebbles rendered smooth by hundred of years of the passage of running water. Often, a forktail could be seen hopping from one rock to another. It was a silent bird, pursuing dragonflies that hovered over the sunlit stream. Not so silent were the magpies, who gossiped in the overhanging branches of willows, water-wood, and walnut. And in the brambles, the wild raspberry and blackberry bushes, small birds—wagtails and finches—made merry.

On a knoll above the stream was a lone pine tree, and sometimes I would recline beneath it, notebook and ballpoint pen at hand, and write a poem or part of a story or a 'remembrance of things past'. But I was no Proust. My mentors were Thoreau and Richard Jefferies. *Walden* and *The Story of My Heart* were often my companions.

To write a poem upon a grassy knoll, with a zephyr, a gentle breeze, playing in the branches of pine, is to live the poem even as you write it. And today, looking back over the years, I can hear the breeze and feel it, and listen to the sound of the stream, the song of the forest, and it is the poem of all my days.

∽

And sometimes, late in the evening, as the full moon rose over the summit of Landour, silhouetting the deodars, I would go out for one of my nocturnal walks, and then the sounds would be more muted, more secretive. An owl talking to himself in the depths of an old oak tree. A nightjar making an occasional comment, like a tap on a table.... A barking deer. Something urgent, frantic about its call tonight. It is on the run from a predator.

Presently I hear the sawing cough of a leopard. It is not an animal that roars in order to intimidate. Like most cats, big or small, it is a silent pursuer. Even so, that cough is a distinctive one.

My balcony light is on. From my window I can see the garden at the rear of the cottage. No porcupines about; my dahlia bulbs are safe. But darting into the garden is the terrified barking deer. It runs here and there, looking for a hiding place, then dashes into my woodshed and stands trembling behind a stack of firewood. Will it be safe there?

Leopards were made to hunt and devour their prey; but tonight I am on the side of the helpless deer. I have no gun, being averse to such abominations. But I can make enough noise to scare the leopard away. There are some firecrackers in a cupboard. I light a string of crackers and toss them into the garden. They rattle away like a machine gun, shattering the silence of the forest.

Has the leopard gone away? I have no idea. But presently that barking deer slips out of its place of refuge and darts into a thicket of dog roses. There are no sounds of a struggle. Perhaps it is safe for the night; for this one night, anyway.

∽

I have been in the cottage for three or four years when one day a predator far more dangerous than the leopard arrives on the scene. It is the P. W. D.'s road-building crew, and they have the authority to build a road right through the front garden, in order to link up with another more important road further along the mountains. They have come equipped with explosives, bulldozers, and an army of road workers. I have to move. And so must some of the forest. Oaks, walnuts, pines, maples, all fall to the axe and the electric saw. The birds go elsewhere. Small animals migrate. Even the porcupines abandon the garden, for the dahlias and gladioli have vanished.

I move higher up the mountain. More roads. You can't escape them. I find a small apartment, part of a larger building overlooking the main road, the road to the summit, Lal Tibba. There's plenty of forest up there, but here it's all road, with scores, nay, hundreds of cars from Delhi, Haryana, and Punjab labouring up the hill, honking and tooting, all in a hurry to get a view of the eternal snows. They won't see much unless they get up very early. By noon, cloud and mist have obscured the higher ranges. I hear a tourist from Punjab complaining to his guide: 'You brought us all the way up here, and what did we see? A kabristan, a cemetery!' He was referring to the old Landour cemetery on the north face of the mountain. It has the best view of the snows. But only the old caretaker enjoys the view. The occupants of the graves are still sleeping.

∽

At night the visitors and the cars have gone, the road below is silent except for a dog howling at the moon. It's a warm night and my window is open. The lights are out. Presently a firefly, a jugnu, floats into my bedroom on the night breeze. It moves around, lighting up little spaces. I haven't seen a firefly since I left the old cottage.

It's like a visit from an old friend; a tiny star come down to see me in the still of the night.

I feel as though it's summoning me back to my old haunts.

I am too old now to walk to the singing forest, but I will pay homage to it in my own way, with these—my written words. And, in the meantime, keep coming little firefly!

GUESTS WHO COME IN FROM THE FOREST

When mist fills the Himalayan valleys, and heavy monsoon rain sweeps across the hills, it is natural for wild creatures to seek shelter. Any shelter is welcome in a storm—and sometimes my cottage in the forest is the most convenient refuge.

There is no doubt that I make things easier for all concerned by leaving most of my windows open. I am one of those peculiar people who like to have plenty of fresh air indoors—and if a few birds, beasts, and insects come in too, they're welcome, provided they don't make too much of a nuisance of themselves.

I must confess that I did lose patience with a bamboo beetle who blundered in the other night and fell into the water jug. I rescued him and pushed him out of the window. A few seconds later he came whirring in again, and with unerring accuracy landed with a plop in the same jug. I fished him out once more and offered him the freedom of the night. But attracted no doubt by the light and warmth of my small sitting room, he came buzzing back, circling the room like a helicopter, looking for a good place to land. Quickly I covered the water jug. He landed in a bowl of wild dahlias, and I allowed him to remain there, comfortably curled up in the hollow of a flower.

Sometimes, during the day, a bird visits me—a deep purple whistling thrush, hopping about on long dainty legs, peering to the right and left, too nervous to sing. She perches on the windowsill, looking out at the rain. She does not permit any familiarity. But if I sit quietly in my chair, she will sit quietly on her windowsill, glancing quickly at me now and then just to make sure that I'm keeping my distance. When the rain stops, she glides away, and it is only then, confident in her freedom, that she bursts into full-throated song, her broken but haunting melody echoing down the ravine.

A squirrel comes sometimes; when his home in the oak tree gets waterlogged. Apparently he is a bachelor; anyway, he lives alone. He knows me well, this squirrel, and is bold enough to climb on to the dining table looking for tidbits which he always finds, because I leave them there deliberately. Had I met him when he was a youngster, he would have learnt to eat from my hand, but I have only been here a few months. I like it this way. I am not looking for pets: these are simply guests.

Last week, as I was sitting down at my desk to write a long-deferred article, I was startled to see an emerald-green praying mantis sitting on my writing pad. He peered up at me with his protuberant glass-bead eyes; and I stared down at him through my reading glasses. When I gave him a prod, he moved off in a leisurely way. Later I found him examining the binding of Whitman's *Leaves of Grass;* perhaps he had found a succulent bookworm. He disappeared for a couple of days, and then I found him again on the dressing table, preening himself before the mirror. Perhaps I am doing him an injustice in assuming that he was preening. Maybe he thought he'd met another mantis and was simply trying to make contact. Anyway, he seemed fascinated by his reflection.

Out in the garden, I spotted another mantis, perched on the jasmine bush. Its arms were raised like a boxer's. Perhaps they're a pair, I thought, and went indoors and fetched my mantis and placed him on the jasmine bush, opposite his fellow insect. He did not like what he saw—no comparison with his own image!—and made off in a huff.

My most interesting visitor comes at night, when the lights are still burning—a tiny bat who prefers to fly in through the door, should it be open, and will use the window only if there's no alternative. His object in entering the house is to snap up the moths that cluster around the lamps.

All the bats I've seen fly fairly high, keeping near the ceiling as far as possible, and only descending to ear level (my ear level) when they must; but this particular bat flies in low, like a dive bomber, and does acrobatics amongst the furniture, zooming in and out of chair legs and under tables. Once, while careening about the room in this fashion, he passed straight between my legs.

Has his radar gone wrong, I wondered, or is he just plain crazy?

I went to my shelves of *Natural History* and looked up bats, but could find no explanation for this erratic behaviour. As a last resort, I turned to an ancient volume,

Sterndale's *Indian Mammalia* (Calcutta, 1884), and in it, to my delight, I found what I was looking for:

> a bat found near Mussoorie by Captain Hutton, on the southern range of hills at 5500 feet; head and body, 1.4 inch; skims close to the ground, instead of flying high as bats generally do; habitat, Jharipani, N.W. Himalayas.

Apparently the bat was rare even in 1884.

Perhaps I've come across one of the few surviving members of the species: Jharipani is only two miles from where I live. And I feel rather offended that modern authorities should have ignored this tiny bat; possibly they feel that it is already extinct. If so, I'm pleased to have rediscovered it. I am happy that it survives in my small corner of the woods, and I undertake to celebrate it in verse:

> Most bats fly high,
> Swooping only
> To take some insect on the wing;
> But there's a bat I know
> Who flies so low
> He skims the floor.
> He does not enter at the window
> But flies in at the door,
> Does stunts beneath the furniture—
> Is his radar wrong,
> Or does he just prefer
> Being different from other bats?

And when sometimes
He settles upside down
At the foot of my bed, I let him be.
On lonely nights, even a crazy bat
Is company.

THE LAST DAYS OF THE TONGA

Tongas, along with tramcars, haircuts, and the Indian rhinoceros, will soon be extinct. In many towns where, ten years ago, there were two or three hundred tongas on the roads, there are now some twenty or thirty. Buses, taxis, above all the ubiquitous scooter-rickshaw, are slowly but surely putting the pony-drawn carriage out of business and out of existence.

This is nowhere more apparent than in Delhi. During World War II, when I was a small boy, the Delhi tonga was the accepted mode of conveyance for high-ranking officers and officials, and for their wives and families.

My father and I thought nothing of taking a tonga from Humayun Road to Connaught Place in order to visit a cinema or Davico's restaurant. There was no bus service then, cars were few, the scooter had not been invented, and the only public transport, the tramcar (now obsolete), plied exclusively in Chandni Chowk and its environs.

In today's Delhi, no one of any standing would think of taking a tonga; it would be *infra dig.* And if a foreign tourist should find a tonga ride exhilarating, we look on him with the tolerant amusement reserved for eccentrics.

This is all very sad for those who, like this writer, have grown up in a tonga-driven world.

When I was very small, I travelled some thirty miles from Dehradun to Haridwar in a tonga. There were a few cars about in those days—it was only twenty-five years ago—but a tonga was considered just as good, almost as fast, and certainly more dependable when it came to crossing the Song River, a small tributary of the Ganga.

During the rains, when the river flowed strong and deep, it was impossible to get across except by a hand-operated ropeway (which is still in use in some areas); but during the dry months, when the river was a small stream, the tonga-pony went splashing through, carriage wheels churning through the clear mountain water. If the pony found the going difficult, we removed our shoes, rolled up our trousers, and waded across, while the driver led his pony by the nuzzle.

Long before my time, in fact before the turn of the century, when the 'Scinde, Panjab, and Delhi railway' went no further than Saharanpur, the only way of getting to Dehra was by the 'night mail', better known as the dak-ghari.

Dak-ghari ponies were difficult animals, always attempting to turn around and get into the carriage with the passengers. It was only when the coachman used his whip liberally, and reviled the ponies' ancestors as far back as their third and fourth generations, that the beasts could be persuaded to move. And once they started, there was no stopping them; it was a gallop all the way to the first stage, where the ponies were changed to the accompaniment of a bugle blown by the coachman in true Dickensian fashion.

The journey through the Siwaliks really began—as it still does today—at the Mohand Pass. This ascent starts with a gradual gradient, which increases as the road becomes more steep and winding. The hills are abrupt and perpendicular on the southern side, but slope gently away to the north.

At this stage of the journey, drums were beaten (if it was day) and torches were lit (if it was night) because sometimes wild elephants resented the approach of the dak-ghari and, trumpeting a challenge, would throw the ponies into confusion and panic, and send them racing back to the plains.

And now the tonga is nearing extinction. With the emergence of a fairly prosperous middle class in many cities, the machine has taken precedence as a means of conveyance. Trucks, buses, cars, motorcycles, and scooters now ply on routes that were once the monopoly of cycles and tongas. If this can be taken as a measure of a country's progress, then we have certainly forged ahead; but our roads, never meant for such heavy traffic, are frequently cracking up.

Tongas are still to be found, but they are usually confined to roads where buses and taxis do not penetrate. Most tonga drivers refuse to change with the times, despite a diminishing income. Their ponies seem to have more traffic sense than some of our taxi drivers, and are involved in fewer accidents.

But give a tonga a straight clear stretch of road, and it will go into action, racing at breackneck speed while the passengers cling to their seats for dear life, and the exhilarated driver, shouting his challenge to the machine age, cracks his whip, calls an endearment to his pony, and bursts into song.

Tonga drivers vary according to the towns they belong to. In Lucknow they are courteous, garrulous, self-styled descendants of nawabs. In Delhi they are aggressive, shrewd, matching the temper of the city. Some of them are selling their ponies and buying scooters. Everywhere, tongas are fading away, becoming part of our nostalgia for the past.

TIGERS FOR DINNER

JUNGLE COOK

My favourite stories as a child?

Well, it would be hard to beat the tales—short or tall—that I heard from Mehmoud, who was our khansama, or cook, when I was five or six years old.

My parents didn't tell me many stories. Mum was busy with her parties and Dad with his stamp collection; that is, when he wasn't in his office. I had the house and the grounds to myself, but there was no one to talk to except the flowers. The cosmos were good listeners. They nodded politely when I spoke to them. The roses looked away; they were very snobbish. The marigolds were friendly enough, provided I didn't pick them.

So I would wander into the kitchen to see what Mehmoud was making for lunch. And to taste the kofta curry or the pulao rice, just to make sure the taste was right. Since then, I've been a curry taster all my life.

Mehmoud was a good cook and, in many ways, my best friend (there being no children on the premises); but he was also a great storyteller.

You see, before coming to us, he'd worked for Jim Corbett, the great shikari, who'd shot a great number of man-eating tigers apart from other dangerous denizens of the jungle.

'Did you see him shoot a tiger?' I asked.

'Oh, many times,' said Mehmoud. 'A tiger a week—that was nothing to Carpet-sahib!'

'Did the tigers come to the house, or did you go looking for them?'

'Carpet-sahib went after them. Most of the time we were in the camps and I had to do my cooking in the open. Not an easy job being a jungle cook. Usually the salt was missing and everyone would complain.'

'My mother says you put too much salt in the food.'

'That's so I don't forget it. Better a salty dish than a tasteless one. Don't you agree, baba?'

'And too many chillies,' I added.

'A chilli a day keeps the doctor away. That's what my grandfather used to say, and he was an Unani physician—a doctor of natural medicine from the old Persian system. A little masala, a little turmeric—and you won't need a medic! My grandfather was a wise man, he taught me to read and write in Urdu, but I never went to school—had to earn a living from a very young age. So I learnt to cook—it's not a bad way of making a living.'

'You're not a bad cook.'

'So tell your parents to increase my salary.'

'Then be careful with the salt.'

'You're a salty boy. And saucy. Try one of these koftas. I knew you'd come, so I made an extra kofta.'

'Thank you, Mehmoud. But tell me about Corbett. And tigers. Did you see a tiger?'

'Of course, I did. There were tigers all over the place. Bang, bang, bang! Carpet-sahib kept firing, and the tigers kept falling. Man-eaters, cattle-eaters, child-eaters. One of them took my masalchi when we were in camp. Took him from the tent we were sharing. Dragged him out by his feet and carried him away while he screamed. That tiger was too fast for Carpet-sahib. By the time the camp roused, both tiger and masalchi had vanished. We found his bones in the morning.'

'What's a masalchi?' I asked.

'The boy who helped me. He helped me prepare the meat and vegetables and washed all the dishes afterwards. He was a big loss. For two weeks I had to manage everything on my own. We couldn't get another masalchi. No applications. And I had to sleep alone for the rest of the time we were in camp. Carpet-sahib told me to keep a fire burning outside my tent. Tigers stay away from fire. They don't like getting burnt.'

'And did it stay away?'

'No, the brute came again. Stuck its head in at the tent opening, looking for another juicy masalchi. But I was ready for it. I had just been frying some eggs, and my frying pan was as hot as hellfire, and with it I struck the tiger on its nose!'

'You're a brave man, Mehmoud. What did the tiger do?'

'It didn't like it. You see, tigers have very sensitive noses. That's why they have such a strong sense of smell. Their noses lead them to their prey. But a burnt nose can be very painful, especially for a tiger. And I'd singed its whiskers too. Tigers don't like losing their whiskers, just like army generals!'

'So what happened?'

'It let out a roar, leapt into the air, fell backwards into the fire, let out another roar, and fled into the jungle. For an hour or more we could hear it roaring with agony.'

'You were very brave, Mehmoud. What did everyone say when you told them what you had done?'

'They didn't believe me, baba. They said I was making it all up; that the tiger had taken off after burning its paw in the fire. I showed Carpet-sahib the tiger's whiskers stuck to the bottom of my frying pan, but he only laughed and said I could serve tiger soup for dinner.'

'But you were a hero, Mehmoud!'

'Yes, baba, I'm glad you think so. Have another kofta.'

EXCITING ENCOUNTERS

The following day, Mehmoud was making lamb chops. I liked lamb chops. Mehmoud knew I liked them, and he had an extra chop ready for me, just in case I felt like a pre-lunch snack.

'What was Jim Corbett's favourite dish?' I asked, while dealing with the succulent chop.

'Oh, he liked roast duck. Used to shoot them as they flew up from the jheel.'

'What's a jheel, Mehmoud?'

'A shallow sort of lake. In places you could walk about in the water. Different types of birds would come there in the winter—ducks and geese and all kinds of baglas—herons, you call them. The baglas are not good to eat, but the ducks make a fine roast.

'So we camped beside the jheel and lived on roast duck for a week until everyone was sick of it.'

'Did you go swimming in the jheel?'

'No, it was full of muggers—those long-nosed crocodiles—they'll snap you up if you come within their range! Nasty creatures, those muggermuch. One of them nearly got me.'

'How did that happen, Mehmoud bhai?'

'Oh, baba, just the memory of it makes me shudder! I'd given everyone their dinner and retired to my tent. It was a hot night and we couldn't sleep. Swarms of mosquitoes rose from the jheel, invaded the tent, and attacked me on the face and arms and feet. I dragged my camp cot outside the tent, hoping the breeze would keep the mosquitoes away. After some time they moved on, and I fell asleep, wrapped up in my bed sheet. Towards dawn, I felt my cot quivering, shaking. Was it an earthquake? But no one else was awake. And then the cot started moving! I sat up, looked about me. The cot was moving steadily forward in the direction of the water. And beneath it, holding us up, was a beastly crocodile!

'It gave me the fright of my life, baba. A muggermuch beneath my bed and I upon it! I cried out for help. Carpet-sahib woke up, rushed out of his tent, his gun in his hands. But it was still dark and all he could see was my bed moving rapidly towards the jheel.

'Just before we struck the water, I leapt from the cot,

and ran up the bank, calling for help. Carpet-sahib saw me then. He ran down the slope, firing at the moving cot. I don't know if he hit the horrible creature, but there was a big splash, and it disappeared into the jheel.'

'And did you recover the cot?'

'No, it floated away and then sank. We did not go after it.'

'And what did Corbett say afterwards?'

'He said I had shown great presence of mind. He said he'd never seen anyone make such a leap for safety!'

'You were a hero, Mehmoud!'

'Thank you, baba. There's time for another lamb chop, if you're hungry.'

'I'm hungry,' I said. 'There's still an hour left to lunchtime. But tell me more about your time with Jim Corbett. Did he like your cooking?'

'Oh, *he* liked it well enough, but his sister was very fussy.'

'He had his sister with him?'

'That's right. He never married, so his sister looked after the household and the shopping and everything connected to the kitchen—except when we were in camp. Then I had a free hand. Carpet-sahib wasn't too fussy about his food, especially when he was out hunting. A sandwich or paratha would keep him going. But if he had guests, he felt he had to give them the best, and then it was hard work for me.

'For instance, there was the Raja of Janakpur, a big, fat man who was very fond of eating—between meals, during meals, and after meals. I don't know why he bothered to come on these shikar trips when he could have stayed at home in his palace and feasted day and night. But he needed trophies to hang on the walls of his palace. You were not considered a great king unless your walls were decorated with the stuffed heads of tigers, lions, antelopes, bears—anything that looked dangerous. The raja could eat and drink all day, but he couldn't go home without a trophy. So he would be hoisted on to an elephant, and sit there in state, firing away at anything that moved in the jungle. He seldom shot anything, but Carpet-sahib would help him out by bringing down a stag or a leopard, and congratulating the raja on his skill and accuracy.

'They weren't all like that, but some of the rajas were stupid or even mad. And the Angrej-sahibs—the English—were no better. They too had to prove their manliness by shooting a tiger or a leopard. Carpet-sahib was always in demand, because he lived at the edge of the jungle and knew where to look for different animals.

'The Raja of Janakpur was safe on an elephant, but one day he made the mistake of walking into the jungle on foot. He hadn't gone far when he met a wild boar running at him. A wild boar may not look very dangerous, but it has deadly tusks and is quick to use them. Before the raja could raise the gun to his shoulder, the pig charged at him. The raja dropped his gun, turned, and ran for his life. But he couldn't run very fast or very far. He tripped and fell, and the boar was almost upon him when I happened along, looking for twigs to make a fire. Luckily, I had a small axe in my hand. I struck the boar over the head. It turned and rammed one of its tusks into my thigh. I struck at it again and again, till it fell dead at my feet. The raja was nowhere in sight.

'As soon as he got into camp, he sent for his servants and made a hurried departure. Didn't even thank me for saving his life.'

'Were you hurt badly, Mehmoud?'

'I was out of action for a few days. The wound took time to heal. My new masalchi did all the cooking, and the food was so bad that most of the guests left in a hurry. I still have the scar. See, baba!'

Mehmoud drew up his pyjamas and showed me a deep scar on his right thigh.

'You were a hero, Mehmoud,' I said. 'You deserved a reward.'

'My reward is here, baba, preparing these lamb chops for you. Come on, have another. Your parents won't notice if they run short at lunch.'

'GOOD SHOT, MEHMOUD!'

It was a long, hot summer that year, but a summer in the plains has its compensations—such as mangoes and melons and litchis and custard apples. The fruit seller came to our house every day, a basket of fresh fruit balanced on his head. One morning, I entered the kitchen to find a bucket full of mangoes, and Mehmoud busy making a large jug of mango milkshake.

'Pass me some ice, baba, you'll find it in the bucket. You can have a milkshake now, and another with your lunch. Carpet-sahib thought highly of my milkshakes. During the mango season, he'd have two glasses of mango milkshake first thing in the morning, and then he'd go out and shoot a tiger!'

'Did you ever shoot a tiger?' I asked, accepting a glass from Mehmoud and adding a chunk of ice to the milkshake.

'I shot a leopard once,' said Mehmoud. 'I wasn't supposed to touch the guns, but one morning, after his milkshake, Carpet-sahib said I could accompany him into the jungle, provided I brought along a large thermos full of mango milkshake. It was a hot, humid morning and Carpet-sahib was soon feeling thirsty.

'"Hold my rifle, Mehmoud, while I have a drink," he said, and he handed me his gun and took the thermos. While he was quenching his thirst, a kakar—a barking deer—appeared in the open, just fifteen to twenty feet in front of us. "Shall I shoot it, sir?" I asked. I'd seen him shooting many times, and I knew how the rifle worked. "Go ahead, old chap," he said. "Let's have some venison for dinner."

'So I put the rifle to my shoulder, took aim, and fired. It was the first time I'd fired a gun, and the butt sprang back and hit me in the shoulder, while the bullet itself whizzed over the deer and into the tree beneath which it was standing.

'Away went the kakar, while I held my shoulder in agony. I'd missed it by several feet. But then there was a terrible groan from the branches of the tree, and a huge leopard came crashing through the foliage, falling with a thud at our feet. It was quite dead, baba.

'I'd missed the kakar and shot a leopard. It must have been watching the deer, waiting to pounce on it, when it was struck by my bullet.

'"Good shot!" cried Carpet-sahib. "Well aimed, Mehmoud, I didn't see the leopard."

'"Nor did I, sir," I said.

'"But you shot it all the same," said Carpet-sahib.

'And since I did not want the skin, he rewarded me with five hundred rupees. The leopard was stuffed and kept on his veranda, to scare away the monkeys. Of course he told everyone what a good shot I was, although it was the last time he asked me to hold his gun.'

'Never mind,' I said, 'you shot the leopard, and you saved the life of the pretty deer. And your mango milkshake is the best in the world.'

'Thank you, baba,' said Mehmoud, refilling my glass. 'This is a good year for mangoes.'

And it was a good year for mango milkshakes. As I discovered.

CROSSING THE ROAD

Samuel was a snail of some individuality. Some considered him to be the bad snail in the family, but that was because he did not listen to his elders and liked to do things in his own way, trying out new plants or venturing into forbidden places. Birds and butterflies recognized no man-made borders, so why should snails? They'd been around longer than humans and were likely to be around even longer.

Not that Samuel had any global ambitions. It was just that the cabbage patch in which he and his fellow snails had been living did not appeal to him any more. He was heartily sick of cabbage leaves. And just across a busy road—his international boundary—was a field full of delicious looking lettuce. And any snail would prefer lettuce to cabbage.

The trouble was, it was a very busy road, linking one city to another, and on it flowed a constant stream of cars, trucks, motorcycles, bicycles, vans, even the occasional steamroller. Samuel did not like the idea of being crushed under a steamroller. There were better ways of exiting planet Earth—being swallowed by a large stork, for instance.

And then, of course, snails can't run. With the help of

a little of their own juices, they glide slowly and leisurely over grass and weed and pebbles, in search of a juicy leaf or the company of a fellow snail. They were not made to run. They are not predators like the larger carnivores. Nor do they prey on each other like humans. They are all for minding their own business. And now here was Samuel, making it his business to invade that lettuce patch on the other side of the road.

Well, nothing ventured, nothing gained. And ignoring the warnings of friends and familiars, Samuel set out to cross that life-threatening road. He could, of course, have waited until it was dark, but the road would have been no safer then. A constant stream of container trucks came thundering down the highway all through the night.

Tentacles waving, he began his stately crawl across the road.

Almost immediately he was nearly run over by a boy on a bicycle. Instinctively, Samuel withdrew into his little shell. Not that it would have made any difference. It might have protected him from a small bird, but not from a cycle tyre.

Samuel looked up and down the road. It was a single width road, and vehicles could approach from either direction. It appeared to be clear at the moment.

Samuel advanced, covering a distance of some twelve inches in sixty seconds flat.

Then—*woosh*—a car sped by, its tyres missing Samuel by inches. He was almost blown away by a cloud of dust and exhaust fumes.

And then came another car. Samuel cringed. And

survived. And wondered if he should turn around and go back the way he came. But snails aren't great thinkers. The lettuce patch was all that mattered.

Samuel had advanced by two or three feet when there came a deep rumbling sound and he felt the ground quiver beneath him. A huge truck was bearing down on him!

Sometimes it is an advantage to be small. Samuel was somewhere in the middle of the road, and nowhere near the wheels when the truck thundered over him. All the same he was dazed and shaken, unable to move any further. Soon another truck would be coming along. Or was it a tractor that was chugging along towards him?

Just then there was a squeal of brakes, a blare of horns, and a tremendous crash. The truck had hit an oncoming car and both had veered off the road and were lying in a ditch. For a time all traffic ceased. Samuel emitted a slimy jet and began to crawl again. Then there was a burst of activity.

A motorcycle came tearing down the road, whizzing past a bewildered Samuel, and then stopping at the accident site. A policeman dismounted. In the distance a siren wailed. An ambulance was on its way.

And then it began to rain, a gentle patter on the tarmac. Refreshed, Samuel slid forward. The rain came down harder, and a fallen peepul leaf came sailing towards Samuel. It stopped beside him and Samuel crawled to the leaf. A spurt of rainwater picked up the leaf and sent it sailing across the remainder of the road and on to the grass verge.

Excelsior!

Samuel was home if not dry.

The lettuce field stretched before him. Motor horns and ambulance sirens melted into the distance. Humans could take care of themselves. So could snails! It would take him weeks to munch his way through a small corner of that lettuce patch, but he was going to try. To the winner the spoils!

The rain stopped and he began his feast.

The lettuce was all right, but it wasn't much better than the cabbage field he had left a little over an hour ago. Had the journey been worthwhile? Could he cross that road again? The odds were against survival.

He'd just have to settle down in this new and unfamiliar world. The grass is always greener on the other side—until you get there!

CHOCOLATES AT MIDNIGHT

One of the great pleasures of life is the afternoon siesta. In Mexico and other Latin American countries it has been perfected to a fine art. In warm countries like ours it is almost a necessity, especially for a farmer toiling in his fields from daybreak to noon. An afternoon nap under a peepul tree or in the shade of a mighty banyan does wonders for body and soul.

I take my siesta on the same bed that I sleep upon at midnight; but if I am travelling I have no difficulty in taking a nap on a plane or in a bus or in a railway waiting room, although I must admit that it's been many years since I travelled by train. Under a tree sounds romantic, but the last time I tried sleeping under a friendly horse chestnut I was woken by chestnuts falling on my head.

Bed is best, especially on a cold winter's day in the hills. And, at night, a hot-water bottle helps.

Given a warm bed, I sleep like a baby. But like a baby I am inclined to wake up at midnight or at one in the morning, feeling rather hungry. And for this purpose I keep a bar of chocolate on my bedside table.

There's nothing like a chunk of chocolate in the middle of the night. It helps me feel that all's right with the world, and I fall asleep again to dream of cricket bats made of chocolate and rainbows made of sugar candy. You must try it sometime, those of you who find difficulty in sleeping.

But a few nights ago I woke up prematurely to hear something nibbling away on my bedside table. *Katr-katr, katr-katr*, came the ominous sound.

I switched on the bedside lamp, and there sat a fat rat, nibbling away at my chocolate!

Now I am generous with most things, and I am happy to share my chocolates with you, gentle reader, but I draw the line at rodents. So I flung a slipper at the rat, who dodged it and took off with some reluctance, and then I had to throw away the remains of the chocolate for fear of catching rat fever or something horrible.

Anyway, the next night I kept a fresh chocolate bar in a drawer of the dressing table, where I felt sure it would be safe. Once again, my dreams were interrupted by the nibble and crunch of small teeth embedding themselves in my chocolate bar. I sprang out of bed, rushed to the dressing table, pulled out the drawer, and out popped Master Rat, the champion chocolate-eater! Away he went, leaving behind only half a bar of chocolate for yours truly.

Apparently he'd found a hole in the back of the drawer, and spurred on by greed, had burrowed his way to the object of his desire.

A trap! A trap was what I needed. So I borrowed my neighbour's rat trap—not the kind that kills, but the kind that imprisons (which may be worse)—and set it up with my favourite chocolate as bait. They say rats prefer cheese, but I wasn't taking any chances.

Anyway, the trap worked, and in the morning I found a disgruntled rat staring at me through the bars of his prison like the Prisoner of Zenda. Picking up the trap, I walked with it for half a mile up the road, and then released Master Rat in the bushes behind a popular bakery. Very irresponsible of me, but I thought the precincts of the bakery would at least keep him occupied.

Three peaceful nights passed. Once again, I enjoyed my midnight chocolate snack. Then—*katr, katr, katr*.... He was back again!

'Once more into the breach, dear friends.' Another trap was borrowed and Master Rat was jailed for a second time. And this time I was taking no chances. I engaged a taxi, drove to the Kempty Waterfall with the rat in its trap. And there flung the protesting rat into the waterfall, much as the villainous Moriarty had flung poor Sherlock Holmes over another waterfall. The last I saw of the rat, he was swimming strongly downstream towards the Yamuna Bridge.

Peace at last. Chocolates forever! Dreams of candyfloss and golden syrups....

And then: *katr, katr, katr*....

I switched on the bedside light.

Two rats were on my desk, having a tug of war with my chocolate bar.

There's only one thing to do.

I'll give up eating chocolates. I'll starve those rats out

of existence, even if, in the process, I must suffer from extreme malnutrition.

Later: I have compromised by eating my chocolates in the daytime.

CRICKET FOR THE CROCODILE

R anji was up at dawn.
It was Sunday, a school holiday. Although he was supposed to be preparing for his exams, only a fortnight away, he couldn't resist one or two more games before getting down to history and algebra and other unexciting things.

'I'm going to be a test cricketer when I grow up,' he told his mother. 'Of what use will maths be to me?'

'You never know,' said his mother, who happened to be more of a cricket fan than his father. 'You might need maths to work out your batting average. And as for history, wouldn't you like to be a part of history? Famous cricketers make history!'

'Making history is all right,' said Ranji. 'As long as I don't have to remember the date on which I make it!'

∽

Ranji met his friends and teammates in the park. The grass was still wet with dew, the sun only just rising behind the distant hills. The park was full of flower beds and swings and slides for smaller children. The boys would have to play on the riverbank against their rivals, the village boys. Ranji did not have a full team that morning, but he was looking for a 'friendly' match. The really important game would be held the following Sunday.

The village team was quite good because the boys lived near each other and practised a lot together, whereas Ranji's team was drawn from all parts of the town. There was the baker's boy, Nathu; the tailor's son, Sunder; the postmaster's son, Prem; and the bank manager's son, Anil. These were some of the better players. Sometimes their fathers also turned up for a game. The fathers weren't very good, but you couldn't tell them that. After all, they helped to provide bats and balls and pocket money.

A regular spectator at these matches was Nakoo, the crocodile, who lived in the river. Nakoo means nosy, but the village boys were very respectful and called him Nakoo-ji, Nakoo sir. He had a long snout, rows of ugly-looking teeth (some of them badly in need of fillings), and a powerful, scaly tail.

He was nearly fifteen feet long, but you did not see much of him; he swam low in the water and glided smoothly through the tall grasses near the river. Sometimes he came out on the riverbank to bask in the sun. He did not care for people, especially cricketers. He disliked the noise they made, frightening away the waterbirds and other creatures required for an interesting menu, and it was also alarming to have cricket balls plopping around in the shallows where he liked to rest.

Once Nakoo crept quite close to the bank manager, who was resting against one of the trees near the riverbank. The bank manager was a portly gentleman, and Nakoo seemed to think he would make a good meal. Just then a party of villagers had come along, beating drums for a marriage party. Nakoo retired to the muddy waters of the river. He was a little tired of swallowing frogs, eels, and herons. That juicy bank manager would make a nice change—he'd grab him one day!

∽

The village boys were a little bigger than Ranji and his friends, but they did not bring their fathers along. The game made very little sense to the older villagers. And when balls came flying across fields to land in milk pails or cooking pots, they were as annoyed as the crocodile.

Today, the men were busy in the fields, and Nakoo was wallowing in the mud behind a screen of reeds and water lilies. How beautiful and innocent those lilies looked! Only sharp eyes would have noticed Nakoo's long snout thrusting above the broad, flat leaves of the lilies. His eyes were slits. He was watching.

Ranji struck the ball hard and high. Splash! It fell into the river about thirty feet from where Nakoo lay. Village boys and town boys dashed into the shallow water to look for the ball. Too many of them! Crowds made Nakoo nervous. He slid away, crossed the river to the opposite bank, and sulked.

As it was a warm day, nobody seemed to want to get out of the water. Several boys threw off their clothes, deciding that it was a better day for swimming than for cricket. Nakoo's mouth watered as he watched those bare limbs splashing about.

'We're supposed to be practising,' said Ranji, who took his cricket seriously. 'We won't win next week.'

'Oh, we'll win easily,' said Anil, joining him on the riverbank. 'My father says he's going to play.'

'The last time he played, we lost,' said Ranji. 'He made two runs and forgot to field.'

'He was out of form,' said Anil, ever loyal to his father, the bank manager.

Sheroo, the captain of the village team, joined them. 'My cousin from Delhi is going to play for us. He made a hundred in one of the matches there.'

'He won't make a hundred on this wicket,' said Ranji. 'It's slow at one end and fast at the other.'

'Can I bring my father?' asked Nathu, the baker's son.

'Can he play?'

'Not too well, but he'll bring along a basket of biscuits, buns, and pakoras.'

'Then he can play,' said Ranji, always quick to make up his mind. No wonder he was the team's captain! 'If there are too many of us, we'll make him twelfth man.'

The ball could not be found, and as they did not want to risk their spare ball, the practice session was declared over.

'My grandfather's promised me a new ball,' said little Mani, from the village team, who bowled tricky leg breaks which bounced off to the side.

'Does he want to play, too?' asked Ranji.

'No, of course not. He's nearly eighty.'

'That's settled, then,' said Ranji. 'We'll all meet here

at nine o'clock next Sunday. Fifty overs a side.'

They broke up, Sheroo and his team wandering back to the village, while Ranji and his friends got on to their bicycles (two or three to a bicycle, since not everyone had one), and cycled back to town.

Nakoo, left in peace at last, returned to his favourite side of the river and crawled some way up the riverbank, as if to inspect the wicket. It had been worn smooth by the players, and looked like a good place to relax. Nakoo moved across it. He felt pleasantly drowsy in the warm sun, so he closed his eyes for a little nap. It was good to be out of the water for a while.

ҫ

The following Sunday morning, a cycle bell tinkled at the gate. It was Nathu, waiting for Ranji to join him. Ranji hurried out of the house, carrying his bat and a thermos of lime juice thoughtfully provided by his mother.

'Have you got the stumps?' he asked.

'Sunder has them.'

'And the ball?'

'Yes. And Anil's father is bringing one too, provided he opens the batting!'

Nathu rode, while Ranji sat on the crossbar with the bat and thermos. Anil was waiting for them outside his house.

'My father's gone ahead on his scooter. He's picking up Nathu's father. I'll follow with Prem and Sunder.'

Most of the boys got to the riverbank before the bank manager and the baker. They left their bicycles under a shady banyan tree and ran down the gentle slope to the river. And then, one by one, they stopped, astonished by what they saw.

They gaped in awe at their cricket pitch. Across it, basking in the soft warm sunshine, was Nakoo the crocodile.

'Where did it come from?' asked Ranji.

'Usually he stays in the river,' said Sheroo, who had joined them. 'But all this week he's been coming out to lie on our wicket. I don't think he wants us to play.'

'We'll have to get him off,' said Ranji.

'You'd better keep out of reach of his tail and jaws!'

'We'll wait until he goes away,' said Prem.

But Nakoo showed no signs of wanting to leave. He rather liked the smooth, flat stretch of ground which he had discovered. And here were all the boys again, doing their best to disturb him.

After some time the boys began throwing pebbles at Nakoo. These had no effect, simply bouncing off the crocodile's tough hide. They tried mud balls and an orange. Nakoo twitched his tail and opened one eye, but refused to move on.

Then Prem took a ball, and bowled a fast one at the crocodile. It bounced just short of Nakoo and caught him on the snout. Startled and stung, he wriggled off the pitch and moved rapidly down the riverbank and into the water. There was a mighty splash as he dived for cover.

'Well bowled, Prem!' said Ranji. 'That was a good ball.' 'Nakoo-ji will be in a bad mood after that,' warned Sheroo. 'Don't get too close to the river.'

The bank manager and the baker were the last to arrive. The scooter had given them some trouble. No one mentioned the crocodile, just in case the adults decided to call the match off.

After inspecting the wicket, which Nakoo had left in fair condition, Sheroo and Ranji tossed a coin. Ranji called 'Heads!' but it came up tails. Sheroo chose to bat first.

The tall Delhi player came out to open the innings with little Mani.

Mani was a steady bat, who could stay at the wicket for a long time; but in a one-day match, quick scoring was needed. This the Delhi player provided. He struck a four, then took a single off the last ball of the over.

In the third over, Mani tried to hit out and was bowled for a duck. So the village team's score was 13 for 1.

'Well done,' said Ranji to fast bowler Prem. 'But we'll have to get that tall fellow out soon. He seems quite good.'

The tall fellow showed no sign of getting out. He hit two more boundaries and then swung one hard and high towards the river.

Nakoo, who had been sulking in the shallows, saw the ball coming towards him. He opened his jaws wide, and with a satisfying 'clunk!' the ball lodged between his back teeth.

Nakoo got his teeth deep into the cricket ball and chewed. Revenge was sweet. And the ball tasted good, too. The combination of leather and cork was just right. Nakoo decided that he would snap up any other balls that came his way.

'Harmless old reptile,' said the bank manager. He produced a new ball and insisted that he bowl with it.

It proved to be the most expensive over of the match. The bank manager's bowling was quite harmless and the Delhi player kept hitting the ball into the fields for fours and sixes. The score soon mounted to 40 for 1. The bank manager modestly took himself off.

By the time the tenth over had been bowled, the score had mounted to 70. Then Ranji, bowling slow spin, lost his grip on the ball and sent the batsman a full toss. Having played the good balls perfectly, the Delhi player couldn't resist taking a mighty swipe at the bad ball. He mistimed his shot and was astonished to see the ball fall into the hands of a fielder near the boundary. 70 for 2. The game was far from being lost for Ranji's team.

A couple of wickets fell cheaply, and then Sheroo came in and started playing rather well. His drives were straight and clean. The ball cut down the buttercups and hummed over the grass. A big hit landed in a poultry yard. Feathers flew and so did curses. Nakoo raised his head to see what all the noise was about. No further cricket balls came his way, and he gazed balefully at a heron who was staying just out of his reach.

The score mounted steadily. The fielding grew slack, as it often does when batsmen gain the upper hand. A catch was dropped. And Nathu's father, keeping wicket, missed a stumping chance.

'No more grown-ups in our team,' grumbled Nathu.

The baker made amends by taking a good catch behind the wicket. The score was 115 for 5, with about half the overs remaining.

Sheroo kept his end up, but the remaining batsmen struggled for runs and the end came with about 5 overs still to go. A modest total of 145.

'Should be easy,' said Ranji.

'No problem,' said Prem.

'Lunch first,' said the bank manager, and they took a half-hour break.

The village boys went to their homes for rest and refreshment, while Ranji and his team spread themselves out under the banyan tree.

Nathu's father had brought patties and pakoras; the bank manager brought a basket of oranges and bananas; Prem had brought a jackfruit curry; Ranji had brought a halwa made from carrots, milk, and sugar; Sunder had brought a large container full of pulao rice cooked with peas and fried onions; and the others had brought various curries, pickles, and sauces. Everything was shared, and with the picnic in full swing no one noticed that Nakoo the crocodile had left the water. Using some tall reeds as cover, he had crept halfway up the riverbank. Those delicious food smells had reached him too, and he was unwilling to be left out of the picnic. Perhaps the boys would leave something for him. If not....

'Time to start,' announced the bank manager, getting up. 'I'll open the batting. We need a good start if we are going to win!'

∽

The bank manager strode out to the wicket in the company of young Nathu. Sheroo opened the bowling for the village team.

The bank manager took a run off the first ball. He puffed himself up and waved his bat in the air as though the match had already been won. Nathu played out the rest of the over without taking any chances.

The tall Delhi player took up the bowling from the other end. The bank manager tapped his bat impatiently, then raised it above his shoulders, ready to hit out. The bowler took a long, fast run up to the bowling crease. He gave a little leap, his arm swung over, and the ball came at the bank manager in a swift, curving flight.

The bank manager still had his bat raised when the ball flew past him and uprooted his middle stump.

A shout of joy went up from the fielders. The bank manager was on his way back to the shade of the banyan tree.

'A fly got in my eye,' he muttered. 'I wasn't ready. Flies everywhere!' And he swatted angrily at flies that no one else could see.

The villagers, hearing that someone as important as a bank manager was in their midst, decided that it would be wrong for him to sit on the ground like everyone else. So they brought him a cot from the village. It was one of those light wooden beds, taped with strands of thin rope. The bank manager lowered himself into it rather gingerly. It creaked but took his weight.

The score was 1 for 1.

Anil took his father's place at the wicket and scored 10 runs in two overs. The bank manager pretended not to notice but he was really quite pleased. 'Takes after me,' he said, and made himself comfortable on the cot.

Nathu kept his end up while Anil scored the runs. Then Anil was out, skying a catch to midwicket.

25 for 2 in six overs. It could have been worse.

'Well played!' called the bank manager to his son, and then lost interest in the proceedings. He was soon fast asleep on the cot. The flies did not seem to bother him any more.

Nathu kept going, and there were a couple of good partnerships for the fourth and fifth wickets. When the Delhi player finished his share of overs, the batsmen became more free in their stroke play. Then little Mani got a ball to spin sharply, and Nathu was caught by the wicketkeeper.

It was 75 for 4 when Ranji came in to bat.

Before he could score a run, his partner at the other end was bowled. And then Nathu's father strode up to the wicket, determined to do better than the bank manager. In this he succeeded by 1 run.

The baker scored 2, and then in trying to run another 2 when there was only one to be had, found himself stranded halfway up the wicket. The wicketkeeper knocked his stumps down.

The boys were too polite to say anything. And as for the bank manager he was now fast asleep under the banyan tree.

So intent was everyone on watching the cricket that no one noticed that Nakoo, the crocodile, had crept further up the riverbank to slide beneath the cot on which the bank manager was sleeping.

There was just room enough for Nakoo to get between the legs of the cot. He thought it was a good place to lie concealed, and he seemed not to notice the large man sleeping peacefully just above him.

Soon the bank manager was snoring gently, and it was not long before Nakoo dozed off, too. Only, instead of snoring, Nakoo appeared to be whistling through his crooked teeth.

∽

75 for 5 and it looked as though Ranji's team would soon be crashing to defeat.

Sunder joined Ranji and, to everyone's delight, played two lovely drives to the boundary. Then Ranji got into his stride and cut and drove the ball for successive fours. The score began to mount steadily. 112 for 5. Once again there were visions of victory.

After Sunder was out, stumped, Ranji was joined by Prem, a big hitter. Runs came quickly. The score reached 140. Only 6 runs were needed for victory.

Ranji decided to do it in style. Receiving a half-volley, he drove the ball hard and high towards the banyan tree.

Thump! It struck Nakoo on the jaw and loosened one of his teeth.

It was the second time that day he'd been caught napping. He'd had enough of it.

Nakoo lunged forward, tail thrashing and jaws snapping. The cot, with the manager still on it, rose with him. Crocodile and cot were now jammed together, and when Nakoo rushed forward, he took the cot with him.

The bank manager, dreaming that he was at sea in a rowing boat, woke up to find the cot pitching violently from side to side.

'Help!' he shouted. 'Help!'

The boys scattered in all directions, for the crocodile was now advancing down the wicket, knocking over stumps and digging up the pitch. He found an abandoned sun hat and swallowed it. A wicketkeeper's glove went the same way. A batsman's pad was caught up on his tail.

All this time the bank manager hung on to the cot for safety, but would he be able to get out of reach of Nakoo's jaw and tail? He decided to hang on to the cot until it was dislodged.

'Come on, boys, help!' he shouted. 'Get me off!'

But the cot remained firmly attached to the crocodile, and so did the bank manager.

The problem was solved when Nakoo made for the river and plunged into its familiar waters. Then the bank manager tumbled into the water and scrambled up the bank, while Nakoo made for the opposite shore.

The bank manager's ordeal was over, and so was the cricket match.

'Did you see how I dealt with that crocodile?' he said, still dripping, but in better humour now that he was safe again. 'By the way, who won the match?'

'We don't know,' said Ranji, as they trudged back to

their bicycles. 'That would have been a 6 if you hadn't been in the way.'

Sheroo, who had accompanied them as far as the main road, offered a return match the following week.

'I'm busy next week,' said the baker.

'I have another game,' said the bank manager.

'What game is that, sir?' asked Ranji.

'Chess,' said the bank manager.

Ranji and his friends began making plans for the next match. 'You won't win without us,' said the bank manager.

'Not a chance,' said the baker.

But Ranji's team did, in fact, win the next match.

Nakoo the crocodile did not trouble them because the cot was still attached to his back, and it took him several weeks to get it off.

A number of people came to the riverbank to look at the crocodile who carried his own bed around.

Some even stayed to watch the cricket.

THE BIG RACE

Dawn crept quietly over the sleeping town. Only a cock was aware of it, and crowed. Koki heard a soft tapping on the windowpane, and immediately sat up in bed. She was ten years old. Her hair fell about her shoulders in a disorderly fashion and there were slight shadows under her dark eyes, but she was wide awake and listening. The tapping was repeated.

Koki got out of bed and tiptoed across to the window and unlatched it. Ranji was standing outside, looking somewhat disgruntled.

'Come on,' he said. 'It's nearly time.'

Koki put her finger to her lips, for she did not want her parents and grandmother to wake up.

'You go and tell Bhim,' she whispered. 'I'll meet you at the maidan.'

Ranji hurried off in the direction of Bhim's house, and Koki turned from the window and went to the dressing table. She combed her hair carelessly and tied it roughly with a ribbon. She was excited and in a hurry, and had slept in her dress, which was very crushed. Now she was ready to leave.

Very quietly, she pulled open a dressing table drawer, and brought out a cardboard box in which were punctured little holes. She opened the lid of the box to see if Rajkumari was all right.

Rajkumari, a dumpy rhino beetle, was asleep on the core of an apple. Koki did not disturb her. She closed the box, and barefoot, crept out of the house through the back door.

As soon as she was outside, Koki broke into a run. She did not stop running until she reached the maidan.

On the maidan, the slanting rays of the early morning sun were just beginning to make emeralds of the dewdrops. Later in the day the grass would dry and be prickly to the feet, but now it was cool and soft. A group of boys had gathered at one corner of the maidan, talking excitedly, and among them were Ranji and Bhim, a lanky, bespectacled boy of fourteen. Koki was the only girl among them.

Bhim's beetle was the favourite for the race. It was a large bamboo beetle, with a slim body and long, slender legs, rather like its master's. It was called 2001. Ranji's beetle was a stone carrier with what looked like a very long pair of whiskers. It was appropriately named Moocha. Koki's beetle was not half as big as the other two. Though she did not know how to tell its sex, she was sure it was a female and had called it Rajkumari.

There were only three entries. Strictly speaking, betting wasn't allowed, but the boys made a few quiet bets among themselves. The prize was a giant insect (there was some disagreement as to whether it was a beetle or an outsized cockroach), which was meant to enable the winner to breed larger racing beetles.

There was some confusion when Ranji's Moocha escaped from his box and took a preliminary canter over the grass; but he was soon caught and returned to his enclosure. Moocha appeared to be in good form; in fact, he would be tough competition for Bhim's 2001.

The course was about two metres long, the tracks fifteen centimetres wide. The tracks were fenced with strips of cardboard so that the contestants did not get in each other's way or leave the course altogether. They were held at the starting post by another piece of cardboard, which would be placed behind them as soon as the race began—just to make sure that no one backed out.

A little Sikh boy in a yellow pyjama-suit was acting as starter, and he kept blowing his whistle for order and attention. When the onlookers saw that the race was about to begin, they fell silent. The little Sikh boy then announced the rules of the race—the contestants were not to be touched during the race, or blown at from behind, or enticed forward with bits of food. They could, however, be cheered on as loudly as anyone wished.

Moocha and 2001 were already at the starting post, but Koki was giving Rajkumari a few words of advice. Rajkumari seemed reluctant to leave her apple core and needed to be taken forcibly to the starting post.

There was further delay when Moocha and 2001 got their horns and whiskers entangled. They had to be separated and calmed down before being placed in their respective tracks. The race was about to start.

Koki knelt on the grass, very quiet and serious, looking from Rajkumari to the finishing line and back again. Ranji was biting his fingernails. Bhim's glasses had clouded over, and he had to keep taking them off and wiping them on his shirt. There was a hush amongst the dozen or so spectators.

'Pee-ee-eeep!' The little Sikh boy blew his whistle.

They were off!

Or rather, Moocha and 2001 were off. Rajkumari was still at the starting post, wondering what had happened to her apple core.

Everyone was cheering madly, and Ranji was jumping up and down, and Bhim's glasses had been knocked off. Moocha was going at a spanking rate. 2001 wasn't taking a great deal of interest in the proceedings, but he was moving, and anything could happen in a race like this.

Koki was on the verge of tears. All the coaching she had given Rajkumari seemed to be of no avail. Her beetle was still looking bewildered and hurt.

'Stop sulking,' said Koki. 'I won't keep you if you don't try.'

Then Moocha stopped suddenly, less than a metre from the finishing line. He seemed to be having trouble with his whiskers, and kept twitching them this way and that. 2001 was catching up slowly but surely, and both Ranji and Bhim were shouting themselves hoarse. Nobody paid any attention to Rajkumari, who was considered to be out of the race; but Koki was using all her willpower to get her racer going.

As 2001 approached Moocha, he seemed to sense his rival's trouble and stopped to find out what was the matter. They could not see each other over the cardboard fence, but otherwise appeared to be communicating very well. Ranji and Bhim were becoming quite frantic in their efforts to rally their faltering steeds, and the cheering on all sides was deafening.

Rajkumari, goaded with rage and frustration at having been deprived of her apple core, now took it into her head to make a bid for liberty and new pastures, and rushed forward in great style.

Koki shouted with joy, but the others did not notice the new challenge until Rajkumari had drawn level with her conferring rivals. There was a gasp from the crowd as Rajkumari strode across the finishing line in record time.

Everyone cheered the gallant outsider. Ranji and Bhim very sportingly shook Koki's hand, congratulating her on Rajkumari's victory. The little Sikh boy in the yellow pyjama-suit blew his whistle for silence and presented Koki with her prize.

Koki gazed in rapture at the new beetle—or was it a cockroach? She stroked its back with her thumb. The insect didn't seem to mind. Then, lest Rajkumari should feel jealous, Koki closed the prize box and, picking up her victorious beetle, returned her to the apple core.

The crowd began to break up. Ranji decided that he would trim Moocha's whiskers before the next race, and Bhim thought 2001 was in need of a special diet.

'Just wait till next Sunday,' said Ranji. 'Then watch my Moocha leave the rest of you standing!'

Bhim said nothing. He looked very thoughtful. There were some new training methods which he was going to try out for next time.

Koki walked home, a cardboard box under each arm. Her thoughts were busy with the future. She would breed beetles (or would they be cockroaches?) until she had a stable of about twenty. Her racers would win every event, both here and in the next town. They might make her famous. Beetle racing would become a national sport!

Meanwhile, she was happy, and Rajkumari was happy on the apple core, and the new insect was just being an insect and did not know and did not care about anything except how to get out of that wretched box.

THE REGIMENTAL MYNA

In my grandfather's time, British soldiers stationed in India were very fond of keeping pets, and there were few barrack rooms where pets were not to be found. Dogs and cats were the most common, but birds were also great favourites.

In one instance, a bird was not only the pet of a barrack room but of a whole regiment. His owner was my grandfather, Private Bond, a soldier of the line who had come out to India with the King's Own Scottish Rifles.

The bird was a myna, common enough in India, and Grandfather named it Dickens after his favourite author. Dickens came into Grandfather's possession when quite young, and he was soon a favourite with all the men in the barracks at Meerut, where the regiment was stationed. Meerut was hot and dusty; the curries were hot and spicy; the General in command was hot-tempered and crusty. Keeping a pet was almost the sole recreation for the men in barracks.

Because he was tamed so young, Dickens (or Dicky for short) never learned to pick up food for himself. Instead, just like a baby bird, he took his meals from Grandfather's mouth. And other men used to feed him in the same way. When Dickens was hungry, he asked for food by sitting on Grandfather's shoulders, flapping his wings rapidly, and opening his beak.

Dicky was never caged, and as soon as he was able to fly he attended all parades, watched the rations being issued, and was present on every occasion which brought the soldiers out of their barracks. When out in the country, he would follow the regiment or party, flying from shoulder to shoulder, or from tree to tree, always keeping a sharp lookout for his enemies, the hawks.

Sometimes he would choose a mounted officer as a companion; but after the manoeuvres were over he would return to Grandfather's shoulder.

One day there was to be a General's inspection, and the Colonel gave orders that Dicky was to be confined, so that he wouldn't appear on parade.

'Lock him away somewhere, Bond,' the Colonel snapped. 'We can't have him flapping all over the parade ground.'

Dickens was put into a storeroom, with the windows closed and the door locked. But while the General's inspection was going on, the mess orderly, who wanted something from the storeroom and knew where to find the key, opened the door.

Out flew Dickens. He made straight for the parade ground, greatly excited at being let out and chattering loudly.

Dicky must have thought the General had something to do with his detention, or else he may have felt an explanation was due to him. Whatever his reasoning, he chose to alight on the General's pith helmet, between the plumes.

Here he chattered faster than ever, much to the surprise of the General, who was obliged to take his helmet off before he could dislodge the bird.

'What the dickens!' exclaimed the General, going purple in the face—for Dicky had discharged his breakfast between the plumes of the helmet.

Meanwhile, Dicky had flown to the Colonel's shoulder to make further complaints, to the great delight of the men.

'Fall out, Bond!' the Colonel screamed. 'Take this bird away—for good! I don't want to see it again!'

A crestfallen Private Bond returned to the barracks with Dicky, wondering what to do next. To part with Dicky, or even to cage him, was out of the question.

But Grandfather was not the only one who loved Dickens. He was also highly popular with the entire battalion. In the end, Grandfather decided to ask his Captain to bring him before the Colonel so he could ask forgiveness for Dicky's behaviour.

The Colonel gave Private Bond and his Captain a patient hearing. Then the Colonel consulted his officers and decided that the bird could stay—provided he was taken on as a serving member of the regiment!

Dickens' popularity was not surprising, as he was highly intelligent. He knew the men of his own regiment from those of others, and would only associate with the Scottish Rifles. Even in the drill season, when there were as many as twenty regiments in camp, Dicky never made a mistake.

Dickens had a unique method of getting from one part of the camp to another. Instead of flying over the top of the camp, he would go in stages from tent to tent, flying very low, sheltering in each one, then peeping out and looking carefully for hawks before moving on to the next.

One day Grandfather was admitted to hospital with malaria. Dicky couldn't find him anywhere, and searched and searched all over the camp in great distress. The hospital was a couple of kilometres away from the barracks, and it wasn't until the third day of searching that Dickens finally discovered Grandfather lying there.

From then on, for as long as Grandfather was on the sick list, Dicky spent his time at the hospital. An upturned helmet was placed on a shelf for him near Grandfather's bed, and Dickens spent the night inside it. As soon as Grandfather was discharged from the hospital, Dickens left as well, and never returned, not even for a visit.

In 1888, the regiment got orders to proceed to Calcutta, en route for Burma, where it was to take part in the Chin Lushai Expedition. All pets had to be left behind, and Dickens was no exception.

But Dicky had his own views on the subject.

The regiment travelled in stages, marching along the Grand Trunk Road, moving at night and going into rest camps for the day.

Dickens caught up on the third day. He arrived in camp after a journey of more than three hundred kilometres—dull, dejected, and starving, as he still depended on being fed from Grandfather's mouth.

Route-marching and travelling by train (the railway was just beginning to spread across India), the battalion finally reached Calcutta. From there, contrary to orders, Dickens embarked for Burma along with the soldiers.

On board the ship, Dickens would amuse himself by peeping from the portholes, and flapping from one to the other. He would also go up on deck, and sometimes even took experimental flights out to sea. But one day he was caught in a gale and had such difficulty getting back to the ship that he gave up that kind of adventuring.

Dickens stayed with his regiment all through the expedition and the campaign. Many of his soldier friends lost their lives, but Grandfather and Dickens survived the fighting and returned safely to Calcutta.

Grandfather, now a Corporal, was given six months' home leave, along with the rest of the regiment. This meant sailing home to England.

During the first part of the voyage, Dicky was his usual cheerful self. But when the ship left the Suez Canal, the weather grew cold, and he was no longer to be seen on the yardarms or on the bridge with the captain. He even lost interest in going on deck with Grandfather, preferring to stay with the parrots on the waste deck.

After the ship passed Gibraltar, Dickens went below. He never came on deck again.

Dickens was laid out in a Huntley and Palmer's biscuit tin, and buried at sea. Not, perhaps, with full military honours, but certainly to the sound of Grandfather's bagpipes, playing 'The Last Post'.

THE MONKEYS

I couldn't be sure, next morning, if I had been dreaming or if I had really heard dogs barking in the night and had seen them scampering about on the hillside below the cottage. There had been a golden cocker, a retriever, a Peke, a dachshund, a black Labrador, and one or two nondescripts. They had woken me with their barking shortly after midnight, and had made so much noise that I had got out of bed and looked out of the open window. I saw them quite plainly in the moonlight, five or six dogs rushing excitedly through the bracken and long monsoon grass.

It was only because there had been so many breeds among the dogs that I felt a little confused. I had been in the cottage only a week, and I was already on nodding or speaking terms with most of my neighbours. Colonel Fanshawe, retired from the Indian army, was my immediate neighbour. He did keep a Cocker, but it was black. The elderly Anglo-Indian spinsters who lived beyond the deodars kept only cats. (Though why cats should be the prerogative of spinsters, I have never been able to understand.) The milkman kept a couple of mongrels. And the Punjabi industrialist who had bought a former prince's palace—without ever occupying it—left the property in charge of a watchman who kept a huge Tibetan mastiff.

None of these dogs looked like the ones I had seen in the night.

'Does anyone here keep a Retriever?' I asked Colonel Fanshawe, when I met him taking his evening walk.

'No one that I know of,' he said and gave me a swift, penetrating look from under his bushy eyebrows. 'Why, have you seen one around?'

'No, I just wondered. There are a lot of dogs in the area, aren't there?'

'Oh, yes. Nearly everyone keeps a dog here. Of course, every now and then a panther carries one off. Lost a lovely little terrier myself only last winter.'

Colonel Fanshawe, tall and red-faced, seemed to be waiting for me to tell him something more—or was he just taking time to recover his breath after a stiff uphill climb?

That night I heard the dogs again. I went to the window and looked out. The moon was at the full, silvering the leaves of the oak trees.

The dogs were looking up into the trees and barking. But I could see nothing in the trees, not even an owl.

I gave a shout, and the dogs disappeared into the forest.

Colonel Fanshawe looked at me expectantly when I met him the following day. He knew something about those dogs, of that I was certain; but he was waiting to hear what I had to say. I decided to oblige him.

'I saw at least six dogs in the middle of the night,'

I said. 'A cocker, a retriever, a Peke, a dachshund, a Labrador, and two mongrels. Now, Colonel, I'm sure you must know whose they are.'

The Colonel was delighted. I could tell by the way his eyes glinted that he was going to enjoy himself at my expense.

'You've been seeing Miss Fairchild's dogs,' he said with smug satisfaction.

'Oh, and where does she live?'

'She doesn't, my boy. Died fifteen years ago.'

'Then what are her dogs doing here?'

'Looking for monkeys,' said the Colonel. And he stood back to watch my reaction.

'I'm afraid I don't understand,' I said.

'Let me put it this way,' said the Colonel. 'Do you believe in ghosts?'

'I've never seen any,' I said.

'But you have, my boy, you have. Miss Fairchild's dogs died years ago—a cocker, a retriever, a dachshund, a Peke, a Labrador, and two mongrels. They were buried on a little knoll under the oaks. Nothing odd about their deaths, mind you. They were all quite old, and didn't survive their mistress very long. Neighbours looked after them until they died.'

'And Miss Fairchild lived in the cottage where I stay? Was she young?'

'She was in her mid-forties, an athletic sort of woman, fond of the outdoors. Didn't care much for men. I thought you knew about her.'

'No, I haven't been here very long, you know. But

what was it you said about monkeys? Why were the dogs looking for monkeys?'

'Ah, that's the interesting part of the story. Have you seen the langur monkeys that sometimes come to eat oak leaves?'

'No.'

'You will, sooner or later. There has always been a band of them roaming these forests. They're quite harmless really, except that they'll ruin a garden if given half a chance…. Well, Miss Fairchild fairly loathed those monkeys. She was very keen on her dahlias—grew some prize specimens—but the monkeys would come at night, dig up the plants, and eat the dahlia bulbs. Apparently they found the bulbs much to their liking. Miss Fairchild would be furious. People who are passionately fond of gardening often go off balance when their best plants are ruined—that's only human, I suppose. Miss Fairchild set her dogs on the monkeys whenever she could, even if it was in the middle of the night. But the monkeys simply took to the trees and left the dogs barking.

'Then one day—or rather one night—Miss Fairchild took desperate measures. She borrowed a shotgun and sat up near a window. And when the monkeys arrived, she shot one of them dead.'

The Colonel paused and looked out over the oak trees which were shimmering in the warm afternoon sun.

'She shouldn't have done that,' he said.

'Never shoot a monkey. It's not only that they're sacred to Hindus—but they are rather human, you know. Well, I must be getting on. Good day!' And the Colonel, having ended his story rather abruptly, set off at a brisk pace through the deodars.

I didn't hear the dogs that night. But the next day I saw the monkeys—the real ones, not ghosts. There were about twenty of them, young and old, sitting in the trees munching oak leaves. They didn't pay much attention to me, and I watched them for some time.

They were handsome creatures, their fur a silver-grey, their tails long and sinuous. They leapt gracefully from tree to tree, and were very polite and dignified in their behaviour towards each other—unlike the bold, rather crude red monkeys of the plains. Some of the younger ones scampered about on the hillside, playing and wrestling with each other like schoolboys.

There were no dogs to molest them—and no dahlias to tempt them into the garden.

But that night, I heard the dogs again. They were barking more furiously than ever.

'Well, I'm not getting up for them this time,' I mumbled, and pulled the blanket over my ears.

But the barking grew louder, and was joined by other sounds, a squealing and a scuffling.

Then suddenly, the piercing shriek of a woman rang through the forest. It was an unearthly sound, and it made my hair stand up.

I leapt out of bed and dashed to the window.

A woman was lying on the ground, three or four huge monkeys were on top of her, biting her arms and pulling at her throat. The dogs were yelping and trying to drag the monkeys off, but they were being harried from behind by others. The woman gave another bloodcurdling shriek, and I dashed back into the room, grabbed hold of a small axe and ran into the garden.

But everyone—dogs, monkeys and shrieking woman—had disappeared, and I stood alone on the hillside in my pyjamas, clutching an axe and feeling very foolish.

The Colonel greeted me effusively the following day.

'Still seeing those dogs?' he asked in a bantering tone.

'I've seen the monkeys too,' I said.

'Oh, yes, they've come around again. But they're real enough, and quite harmless.'

'I know—but I saw them last night with the dogs.'

'Oh, did you really? That's strange, very strange.'

The Colonel tried to avoid my eye, but I hadn't quite finished with him.

'Colonel,' I said. 'You never did get around to telling me how Miss Fairchild died.'

'Oh, didn't I? Must have slipped my memory. I'm getting old, don't remember people as well as I used to. But, of course, I remember about Miss Fairchild, poor lady. The monkeys killed her. Didn't you know? They simply tore her to pieces....'

His voice trailed off, and he looked thoughtfully at a caterpillar that was making its way up his walking stick.

'She shouldn't have shot one of them,' he said. 'Never shoot a monkey—they're rather human, you know....'

THE HARE IN THE MOON

A long time ago, when animals could talk, there lived in a forest four wise creatures—a hare, a jackal, an otter, and a monkey.

They were good friends, and every evening they would sit together in a forest glade to discuss the events of the day, exchange advice, and make good resolutions. The hare was the noblest and wisest of the four. He believed in the superiority of men and women, and was always telling his friends tales of human goodness and wisdom.

One evening, when the moon rose in the sky—and in those days the moon's face was clear and unmarked—the hare looked up at it carefully and said: 'Tomorrow good men will observe a fast, for I can see that it will be the middle of the month. They will eat no food before sunset, and during the day they will give alms to any beggar or holy man who may meet them. Let us promise to do the same. In that way, we can come a little closer to human beings in dignity and wisdom.'

The others agreed, and then went their different ways.

Next day, the otter got up, stretched himself, and was preparing to get his breakfast when he remembered the vow he had taken with his friends.

If I keep my word, how hungry I shall be by evening! he thought. I'd better make sure that there's plenty to eat once the fast is over. He set off towards the river.

A fisherman had caught several large fish early that morning, and had buried them in the sand, planning to return for them later. The otter soon smelt them out.

'A supper all ready for me!' he said to himself. 'But since it's a holy day, I mustn't steal.' Instead he called out: 'Does anyone own this fish?'

There being no answer, the otter carried the fish off to his home, setting it aside for his evening meal. Then he locked his front door and slept all through the day, undisturbed by beggars or holy men asking for alms.

Both the monkey and the jackal felt much the same way when they got up that morning. They remembered their vows but thought it best to have something put by for the evening. The jackal found some stale meat in someone's back yard. Ah, that should improve with age, he thought, and took it home for his evening meal. And the monkey climbed a mango tree and picked a bunch of mangoes. Like the otter, they decided to sleep through the day.

The hare woke early. Shaking his long ears, he came out of his burrow and sniffed the dew-drenched grass.

When evening comes, I can have my fill of grass, he thought. But if a beggar or holy man comes my way, what can I give him? I cannot offer him grass, and I have nothing else to give. I shall have to offer myself. Most men seem to relish the flesh of the hare. We're good to eat, I'm told. And pleased with this solution to the problem, he scampered off.

Now the God Sakka had been resting on a cloud not far away, and he had heard the hare speaking aloud.

'I will test him,' said the god. 'Surely no hare can be so noble and unselfish.'

Towards evening, God Sakka descended from his cloud, and assuming the form of an old priest, he sat down near the hare's burrow. When the animal came home from his romp, he said: 'Good evening, little hare. Can you give me something to eat? I have been fasting all day, and am so hungry that I cannot pray.'

The hare, remembering his vow, said: 'Is it true that men enjoy eating the flesh of the hare?'

'Quite true,' said the priest.

'In that case,' said the hare, 'since I have no other food to offer you, you can make a meal of me.'

'But I am a holy man, and this is a holy day, and I may not kill any living creature with my own hands.'

'Then collect some dry sticks and set them alight. I will leap into the flames myself, and when I am roasted you can eat me.'

God Sakka marvelled at these words, but he was still not quite convinced, so he caused a fire to spring up from the earth. The hare, without any hesitation, jumped into the flames.

'What's happening?' called the hare after a while. 'The fire surrounds me, but not a hair of my coat is singed. In fact, I'm feeling quite cold!'

As the hare spoke, the fire died down, and he found himself sitting on the cool sweet grass. Instead of the old priest, there stood before him the God Sakka in all his radiance.

'I am God Sakka, little hare, and having heard your vow, I wanted to test your sincerity. Such unselfishness of yours deserves immortality. It must be known throughout the world.'

God Sakka then stretched out his hand towards the mountain, and drew from it some of the essence which ran in its veins. This he threw towards the moon, which had just risen, and instantly the outline of the hare appeared on the moon's surface.

Then leaving the hare in a bed of sweet grass, he said: 'For ever and ever, little hare, you shall look down from the moon upon the world, to remind men of the old truth, "Give to others, and the gods will give to you."'

THOSE THREE BEARS

Most Himalayan villages lie in valleys where there are small streams, some farmland, and protection from the biting winds that come through the mountain passes in winter. The houses are usually made of large stones and have sloping slate roofs so the heavy monsoon rain can run off easily. During the sunny autumn months, the roofs are often covered with pumpkins, left there to ripen in the sun.

One October night, when I was sleeping at a friend's house in a village in these hills, I was awakened by a rumbling and thumping on the roof. I woke my friend and asked him what was happening.

'It's only a bear,' he said.

'Is it trying to get in?'

'No. It's after the pumpkins.'

A little later, when we looked out a window, we saw a black bear making off through a field, leaving a trail of half-eaten pumpkins.

FACE TO FACE

In winter, when snow covers the higher ranges, the Himalayan bears come to lower altitudes in search of food. Sometimes they forage in fields and, because they are short-sighted and suspicious of anything that moves, they can be dangerous. But, like most wild animals, they avoid humans as much as possible.

Village folk always advise me to run downhill if chased by a bear. They say bears find it easier to run uphill than down. I am yet to be chased by a bear, and will happily skip the experience. But I have seen a few of these mountain bears in India, and they are always fascinating to watch.

Himalayan bears enjoy pumpkins, corn, plums, and apricots. Once, while I was sitting in an oak tree hoping to see a pair of pine martens that lived nearby, I heard the whining grumble of a bear, and presently, a small bear ambled into the clearing beneath the tree.

He was little more than a cub, and I was not alarmed. I sat very still, waiting to see what he would do.

He put his nose to the ground and sniffed his way along until he came to a large anthill. Here he began huffing and puffing, blowing rapidly in and out of his nostrils, so that the dust from the anthill flew in all directions. But the anthill had been deserted, and so, grumbling, the bear made his way up a nearby plum tree. Soon he was perched high in the branches. It was then that he saw me.

The bear at once scrambled several feet higher up the tree and lay flat on a branch. Since it wasn't a very big branch, there was a lot of bear showing on either side. He tucked his head behind another branch. He could no longer see me, so he apparently was satisfied that he was hidden, although he couldn't help grumbling.

Like all bears, this one was full of curiosity. So, slowly, inch by inch, his black snout appeared over the edge of the branch. As soon as he saw me, he drew his head back and hid his face.

He did this several times. I waited until he wasn't looking, then moved some way down my tree. When the bear looked over and saw that I was missing, he was so pleased that he stretched right across to another branch and helped himself to a plum. I couldn't help bursting into laughter.

The startled young bear tumbled out of the tree, dropped through the branches some fifteen feet, and landed with a thump in a pile of dried leaves. He was unhurt, but fled from the clearing, grunting and squealing all the way.

THE FLAG 'BEARER'

Another time, my friend Prem told me, a bear had been active in his cornfield. We took up a post at night in an old cattle shed, which gave a clear view of the moonlit field.

A little after midnight, a female bear came down to the edge of the field. She seemed to sense that we had been about. She was hungry, however. So, after standing on her hind legs and peering around to make sure the field was empty, she came cautiously out of the forest.

Her attention was soon distracted by some Tibetan prayer flags, which had been strung between two trees.

She gave a grunt of disapproval and began to back away, but the fluttering of the flags was a puzzle that she wanted to solve. So she stopped and watched them.

Soon the bear advanced to within a few feet of the flags, examining them from various angles. Then, seeing that they posed no danger, she went right up to the flags and pulled them down. Grunting with apparent satisfaction, she moved into the field of corn.

Prem had decided that he didn't want to lose any more of his crop, so he started shouting. His children woke up and soon came running from the house, banging on empty kerosene tins.

Deprived of her dinner, the bear made off in a bad temper. She ran downhill at a good speed, and I was glad that I was not in her way.

Uphill or downhill, an angry bear is best given a very wide berth.

THE EYES OF THE EAGLE

It was a high, piercing sound, almost like the yelping of a dog. Jai stopped picking the wild strawberries that grew in the grass around him, and looked up at the sky. He had a dog—a shaggy guard dog called Motu—but Motu did not yelp, he growled and barked. The strange sound came from the sky, and Jai had heard it before. Now, realizing what it was, he jumped to his feet, calling to his dog, calling his sheep to start for home. Motu came bounding towards him, ready for a game.

'Not now, Motu!' said Jai. 'We must get the lambs home quickly.' Again he looked up at the sky.

He saw it now, a black speck against the sun, growing larger as it circled the mountain, coming lower every moment—a golden eagle, king of the skies over the higher Himalaya, ready now to swoop and seize its prey.

Had it seen a pheasant or a pine marten? Or was it after one of the lambs? Jai had never lost a lamb to an eagle, but recently some of the other shepherds had been talking about a golden eagle that had been preying on their flocks.

The sheep had wandered some way down the side of the mountain, and Jai ran after them to make sure that none of the lambs had gone off on its own. Motu ran about, barking furiously. He wasn't very good at keeping the sheep together—he was often bumping into them and sending them tumbling down the slope—but his size and bear-like look kept the leopards and wolves at a distance.

Jai was counting the lambs; they were bleating loudly and staying close to their mothers. *One—two—three—four....*

There should have been a fifth. Jai couldn't see it on the slope below him. He looked up towards a rocky ledge near the steep path to the Tung Temple. The golden eagle was circling the rocks.

The bird disappeared from sight for a moment, then rose again with a small creature grasped firmly in its terrible talons.

'It has taken a lamb!' shouted Jai. He started scrambling up the slope. Motu ran ahead of him, barking furiously at the big bird as it glided away over the tops of the stunted junipers to its eyrie on the cliffs above Tung.

There was nothing that Jai and Motu could do except stare helplessly and angrily at the disappearing eagle. The lamb had died the instant it had been struck. The rest of the flock seemed unaware of what had happened. They still grazed on the thick, sweet grass of the mountain slopes.

'We had better drive them home, Motu,' said Jai, and at a nod from the boy, the big dog bounded down the slope to take part in his favourite game of driving the sheep homewards. Soon he had them running all over the place, and Jai had to dash about trying to keep them together. Finally, they straggled homewards.

'A fine lamb gone,' said Jai to himself gloomily. 'I wonder what Grandfather will say.'

Grandfather said, 'Never mind. It had to happen someday. That eagle has been watching the sheep for some time.'

Grandmother, more practical, said, 'We could have sold the lamb for three hundred rupees. You'll have to be more careful in future, Jai. Don't fall asleep on the hillside, and don't read storybooks when you are supposed to be watching the sheep!'

'I wasn't reading this morning,' said Jai truthfully, forgetting to mention that he had been gathering strawberries.

'It's good for him to read,' said Grandfather, who had never had the luck to go to school. In his days, there weren't any schools in the mountains. Now there was one in every village.

'Time enough to read at night,' said Grandmother, who did not think much of the little one-room school down at Maku, their home village.

'Well, these are the October holidays,' said Grandfather. 'Otherwise he would not be here to help us with the sheep. It will snow by the end of the month, and then we will move with the flock. You will have more time for reading then, Jai.'

At Maku, which was down in the warmer valley, Jai's parents tilled a few narrow terraces on which they grew barley, millets, and potatoes. The old people brought their sheep up to the Tung meadows to graze during the summer months. They stayed in a small stone hut just off the path which pilgrims took to the ancient temple. At 12,000 feet above sea level, it was the highest Hindu temple on the inner Himalayan ranges.

The following day Jai and Motu were very careful. They did not let the sheep out of sight even for a minute. Nor did they catch sight of the golden eagle. 'What if it attacks again?' wondered Jai. 'How will I stop it?'

The great eagle, with its powerful beak and talons, was more than a match for boy or dog. Its hind claws, four inches round the curves, were its most dangerous weapon. When it spread its wings, the distance from tip to tip was more than eight feet.

The eagle did not come that day because it had fed well and was now resting in its eyrie. Old bones, which had belonged to pheasants, snow cocks, pine martens, and even foxes, were scattered about the rocks which formed the eagle's home. The eagle had a mate, but it was not the breeding season and she was away on a scouting expedition of her own.

The golden eagle stood on its rocky ledge, staring majestically across the valley. Its hard, unblinking eyes missed nothing. Those strange orange-yellow eyes could spot a field rat or a mouse hare more than a hundred yards below.

There were other eagles on the mountain, but usually they kept to their own territory. And only the bolder ones went for lambs, because the flocks were always protected by men and dogs.

The eagle took off from its eyrie and glided gracefully,

powerfully over the valley, circling the Tung mountain.

Below lay the old temple, built from slabs of grey granite. A line of pilgrims snaked up the steep, narrow path. On the meadows below the peak, the sheep grazed peacefully, unaware of the presence of the eagle. The great bird's shadow slid over the sunlit slopes.

The eagle saw the boy and the dog, but he did not fear them. He had his eye on a lamb that was frisking about on the grass, a few feet away from the other grazing sheep.

Jai did not see the eagle until it swept around an outcrop of rocks about a hundred feet away. It moved silently, without any movement of its wings, for it had already built up the momentum for its dive. Now it came straight at the lamb.

Motu saw the bird in time. With a low growl he dashed forward and reached the side of the lamb at almost the same instant that the eagle swept in.

There was a terrific collision. Feathers flew. The eagle screamed with rage. The lamb tumbled down the slope, and Motu howled in pain as the huge beak struck him high on the leg.

The big bird, a little stunned by the clash, flew off rather unsteadily, with a mighty beating of its wings.

Motu had saved the lamb. It was frightened but unhurt. Bleating loudly, it joined the other sheep, who took up the bleating. Jai ran up to Motu, who lay whimpering on the ground. There was no sign of the eagle. Quickly he removed his shirt and vest; then he wrapped his vest around the dog's wound, tying it in position with his belt.

Motu could not get up, and he was much too heavy for Jai to carry. Jai did not want to leave his dog alone, in case the eagle returned to attack.

He stood up, cupped his hand to his mouth, and began calling for his grandfather.

'Dada, dada!' he shouted, and presently Grandfather heard him and came stumbling down the slope. He was followed by another shepherd, and together they lifted Motu and carried him home.

Motu had a bad wound, but Grandmother cleaned it and applied a paste made of herbs. Then she laid strips of carrot over the wound—an old mountain remedy—and bandaged the leg. But it would be some time before Motu could run about again. By then it would probably be snowing and time to leave these high-altitude pastures and return to the valley. Meanwhile, the sheep had to be taken out to graze, and Grandfather decided to accompany Jai for the remaining period.

They did not see the golden eagle for two or three days, and, when they did, it was flying over the next range. Perhaps it had found some other source of food, or even another flock of sheep. 'Are you afraid of the eagle?' Grandfather asked Jai.

'I wasn't before,' said Jai. 'Not until it hurt Motu. I did not know it could be so dangerous. But Motu hurt it too. He banged straight into it!'

'Perhaps it won't bother us again,' said Grandfather thoughtfully. 'A bird's wing is easily injured—even an eagle's.'

Jai wasn't so sure. He had seen it strike twice, and

he knew that it was not afraid of anyone. Only when it learnt to fear his presence would it keep away from the flock.

The next day Grandfather did not feel well; he was feverish and kept to his bed. Motu was hobbling about gamely on three legs; the wounded leg was still very sore.

'Don't go too far with the sheep,' said Grandmother. 'Let them graze near the house.'

'But there's hardly any grass here,' said Jai.

'I don't want you wandering off while that eagle is still around.'

'Give him my stick,' said Grandfather from his bed. Grandmother took it from the corner and handed it to the boy.

It was an old stick, made of wild cherry wood, which Grandfather often carried around. The wood was strong and well-seasoned; the stick was stout and long. It reached up to Jai's shoulders.

'Don't lose it,' said Grandfather. 'It was given to me many years ago by a wandering scholar who came to the Tung Temple. I was going to give it to you when you got bigger, but perhaps this is the right time for you to have it. If the eagle comes near you, swing the stick around your head. That should frighten it off!'

Clouds had gathered over the mountains, and a heavy mist hid the Tung Temple. With the approach of winter, the flow of pilgrims had been reduced to a trickle. The shepherds had started leaving the lush meadows and returning to their villages at lower altitudes. Very soon the bears and the leopards and the golden eagles would have the high ranges all to themselves.

Jai used the cherry wood stick to prod the sheep along the path until they reached the steep meadows. The stick would have to be a substitute for Motu. And they seemed to respond to it more readily than they did to Motu's mad charges.

Because of the sudden cold and the prospect of snow, Grandmother had made Jai wear a rough woollen jacket and a pair of high boots bought from a Tibetan trader. He wasn't used to the boots—he wore sandals at other times—and had some difficulty in climbing quickly up and down the hillside. It was tiring work, trying to keep the flock together. The cawing of some crows warned Jai that the eagle might be around, but the mist prevented him from seeing very far.

After some time the mist lifted and Jai was able to see the temple and the snow peaks towering behind it. He saw the golden eagle, too. It was circling high overhead. Jai kept close to the flock—one eye on the eagle, one eye on the restless sheep.

Then the great bird stooped and flew lower. It circled the temple and then pretended to go away. Jai felt sure it would be back. And a few minutes later it reappeared from the other side of the mountain. It was much lower now, wings spread out and back, taloned feet to the fore, piercing eyes fixed on its target—a small lamb that had suddenly gone frisking down the slope, away from Jai and the flock.

Now it flew lower still, only a few feet off the ground, paying no attention to the boy.

It passed Jai with a great rush of air, and as it did so the boy struck out with his stick and caught the bird a glancing blow.

The eagle missed its prey, and the tiny lamb skipped away.

To Jai's amazement, the bird did not fly off. Instead it landed on the hillside and glared at the boy, as a king would glare at a humble subject who had dared to pelt him with a pebble.

The golden eagle stood almost as tall as Jai. Its wings were still outspread. Its fierce eyes seemed to be looking through and through the boy.

Jai's first instinct was to turn and run. But the cherry wood stick was still in his hands, and he felt sure there was power in it. He saw that the eagle was about to launch itself again at the lamb. Instead of running away, he ran forward, the stick raised above his head.

The eagle rose a few feet off the ground and struck out with its huge claws.

Luckily for Jai, his heavy jacket took the force of the blow. A talon ripped through the sleeve, and the sleeve fell away. At the same time the heavy stick caught the eagle across its open wing. The bird gave a shrill cry of pain and fury. Then it turned and flapped heavily away, flying unsteadily because of its injured wing.

Jai still clutched the stick because he expected the bird to return; he did not even glance at his torn jacket. But the golden eagle had alighted on a distant rock and was in no hurry to return to the attack.

Jai began driving the sheep home. The clouds

had become heavy and black, and presently the first snowflakes began to fall.

Jai saw a hare go lolloping down the hill. When it was about fifty yards away, there was a rush of air from the eagle's beating wings, and Jai saw the bird approaching the hare in a sidelong drive.

'So it hasn't been badly hurt,' thought Jai, feeling a little relieved, for he could not help admiring the great bird. 'Now it has found something else to chase for its dinner.'

The hare saw the eagle and dodged about, making for a clump of junipers. Jai did not know if it was caught or not, because the snow and sleet had increased and both bird and hare were lost in the gathering snowstorm.

The sheep were bleating behind him. One of the lambs looked tired, and he stooped to pick it up. As he did so, he heard a thin, whining sound. It grew louder by the second. Before he could look up, a huge wing caught him across the shoulders and sent him sprawling. The lamb tumbled down the slope with him, into a thorny bilberry bush.

The bush saved them. Jai saw the eagle coming in again, flying low. It was another eagle! One had been vanquished, and now here was another, just as big and fearless, probably the mate of the first eagle.

Jai had lost his stick and there was no way by which he could fight the second eagle. So he crept further into the bush, holding the lamb beneath him. At the same time he began shouting at the top of his voice—both to scare the bird away and to summon help. The eagle could not easily get at them now; but the rest of the flock was exposed on the hillside. Surely the eagle would make for them.

Even as the bird circled and came back in another dive, Jai heard fierce barking. The eagle immediately swung away and rose skywards.

The barking came from Motu. Hearing Jai's shouts and sensing that something was wrong, he had come limping out of the house, ready to battle. Behind him came another shepherd and—most wonderful of all—Grandmother herself, banging two frying pans together. The barking, the banging, and the shouting frightened the eagles away. The sheep scattered, too, and it was some time before they could all be rounded up. By then it was snowing heavily.

'Tomorrow, we must all go down to Maku,' said the shepherd.

'Yes, it's time we went,' said Grandmother. 'You can read your storybooks again, Jai.'

'I'll have my own story to tell,' said Jai.

When they reached the hut and Jai saw Grandfather, he said, 'Oh, I've forgotten your stick!'

But Motu had picked it up. Carrying it between his teeth, he brought it home and sat down with it in the open doorway. He had decided the cherry wood was good for his teeth and would have chewed it up if Grandmother hadn't taken it from him.

'Never mind,' said Grandfather, sitting up on his cot. 'It isn't the stick that matters. It's the person who holds it.'

COPPERFIELD IN THE JUNGLE

Grandfather never hunted wild animals; he could not understand the pleasure some people obtained from killing the creatures of our forests. Birds and animals, he felt, had as much right to live as humans. There was some justification in killing for food—most animals did—but none at all in killing just for the fun of it.

At the age of twelve, I did not have the same high principles as Grandfather. Nevertheless, I disliked anything to do with shikar or hunting. I found it terribly boring.

Uncle Henry and some of his sporting friends once took me on a shikar expedition into the Terai forests of the Siwaliks. The prospect of a whole week in the jungle as camp follower to several adults with guns filled me with dismay. I knew that long, weary hours would be spent tramping behind these tall, professional-looking huntsmen. They could only speak in terms of bagging this tiger or that wild elephant, when all they ever got, if they were lucky, was a wild hare or a partridge. Tigers and excitement, it seemed, came only to Jim Corbett.

This particular expedition proved to be different from others. There were four men with guns, and at the end of the week, all that they had shot were two miserable, underweight wild fowls. But I managed, on our second day in the jungle, to be left behind at the rest house. And, in the course of a morning's exploration of the old bungalow, I discovered a shelf of books half hidden in a corner of the back veranda.

Who had left them there? A literary forest officer? A memsahib who had been bored by her husband's campfire boasting? Or someone who had no interest in the 'manly' sport of slaughtering wild animals and had brought his library along to pass the time?

Or possibly the poor fellow had gone into the jungle one day, as a gesture towards his more bloodthirsty companions, and been trampled by an elephant, or gored by a wild boar, or (more likely) accidentally shot by one of the shikaris and his sorrowing friends had taken his remains away and left his books behind.

Anyway, there they were—a shelf of some thirty volumes, obviously untouched for many years. I wiped the thick dust off the covers and examined the titles. As my reading tastes had not yet formed, I was willing to try anything. The bookshelf was varied in its contents—and my own interests have since remained fairly universal.

On that fateful day in the forest rest house, I discovered P. G. Wodehouse and read his *Love Among the Chickens*, an early Ukridge story and still one of my favourites. By the time the perspiring hunters came home late in the evening, with their spent cartridges and lame excuses, I had made a start with M. R. James's *Ghost Stories of an Antiquary*, which had me hooked on ghost stories for the rest of my life. It kept me awake most of the night, until the oil in the kerosene lamp had finished.

Next morning, fresh and optimistic again, the shikaris set out for a different area, where they hoped to 'bag a tiger'. They had employed a party of villagers to beat drums in the jungle, and all day I could hear their drums throbbing in the distance. This did not prevent me from finishing M. R. James or discovering a book called *A Naturalist on the Prowl* by Edward Hamilton Aitken.

My concentration was disturbed only once, when I looked up and saw a spotted deer crossing the open clearing in front of the bungalow. The deer disappeared among the sal trees, and I returned to my book.

Dusk had fallen when I heard the party returning from the hunt. The great men were talking loudly and seemed excited. Perhaps they had got their tiger. I put down my book and came out to meet them.

'Did you shoot the tiger?' I asked excitedly.

'No, my boy,' said Uncle Henry. 'I think we'll bag it tomorrow. But you should have been with us—we saw a spotted deer!'

There were three days left and I knew I would never get through the entire bookshelf. So I chose *David Copperfield*—my first encounter with Dickens—and settled down on the veranda armchair to make the acquaintance of Mr Micawber and his family, Aunt Betsey Trotwood, Mr Dick, Peggotty, and a host of other larger-than-life people. I think it would be true to say that *David Copperfield* set me off on the road to literature; I identified with young David and wanted to grow up to be a writer like him.

But on my second day with the book an event occurred which disturbed my reading for a little while.

I had noticed, on the previous day, that a number of stray dogs—belonging to watchmen, villagers, and forest guards—always hung about the house, waiting for scraps of food to be thrown away. It was ten o'clock in the morning, a time when wild animals seldom come into the open, when I heard a sudden yelp in the clearing. Looking up, I saw a large leopard making off into the jungle with one of the dogs held in its jaws. The leopard had either been driven towards the house by the beaters, or had watched the party leave the bungalow and decided to help itself to a meal.

There was no one else about at the time. Since the dog was obviously dead within seconds of being seized, and the leopard had disappeared, I saw no point in raising an alarm which would have interrupted my reading. So I returned to *David Copperfield*.

It was getting late when the shikaris returned. They were dirty, sweaty, and as usual, disappointed. Next day we were to return to the city, and none of the hunters had anything to show for a week in the jungle. Swear words punctuated their conversation.

'No game left in these...jungles,' said the leading member of the party, famed for once having shot two man-eating tigers and a basking crocodile in rapid succession.

'It's this beastly weather,' said Uncle Henry. 'No rain for months.'

'I saw a leopard this morning,' I said modestly.

But no one took me seriously. 'Did you really?' said the leading hunter, glancing at the book beside me. 'Young Master Copperfield says he saw a leopard!'

'Too imaginative for his age,' said Uncle Henry. 'Comes from reading too much, I suppose.'

'If you were to get out of the house and into the jungle,' said the third member, 'you might really see a leopard! Don't know what young chaps are coming to these days.'

I went to bed early and left them to their tales of the 'good old days' when rhinos, cheetahs, and possibly even the legendary phoenix were still available for slaughter.

Next day the camp broke up and we went our different ways. I was still only halfway through *David Copperfield*, but I saw no reason why it should be left behind to gather dust for another thirty years, and so I took it home with me. I have it still, a reminder of how I failed as a shikari but launched myself on a literary career.

OWLS IN THE FAMILY

One morning we found a full-fledged baby spotted owlet on the ground by the veranda steps. When Grandfather picked it up, it hissed and clacked its bill, but, after a meal of raw meat and water, settled down for the day under my bed.

The spotted owlet, even when full grown, is only the size of a myna, and has none of the sinister appearance of the larger owls. A pair of them may often be found in an old mango or tamarind tree, and by tapping on the tree trunk you may be able to persuade the bird to show an enquiring face at the entrance to its hole. The bird is not normally afraid of man, nor is it strictly a night-bird; but it prefers to stay at home during the day, as it is sometimes attacked by other birds, who consider all owls as their enemies.

The little owlet was quite happy under my bed. The following day a second owlet was found in almost the same place on the veranda, and only then did we realize that where the rainwater pipe emerged through the roof, there was a rough sort of nest, from which the birds had fallen. We took the second young owl to join the first, and fed them both. When I went to bed they were on the ledge just inside the mosquito netting, and, later in the night, their mother found them there. From outside she crooned and gurgled for a long time, and in the morning I found that she had left a mouse with its tail tucked through the mosquito net! Obviously, she placed no reliance on me as a foster parent.

The young birds throve and, ten days later at dawn, Grandfather and I took them into the garden to release them. I had placed one on a branch of the mango tree, and was stooping to pick up the other, when I received quite a heavy blow on the back of my head. A second or two later, the mother owl swooped down at Grandfather, but he was agile enough to duck out of its way. Quickly, I placed the second owl under the mango tree. Then, from a safe distance, we watched the mother fly down and lead her offspring into the long grass at the edge of the garden.

We thought she would take her family away from the vicinity of our rather strange household; but next morning, on coming out of my room, I found two young owls standing on the wall just outside the door! I ran to tell Grandfather, and, when we came back, we found the mother sitting on the birdbath ten yards away. She was evidently feeling sorry for her behaviour the previous day, because she greeted us with a soft 'whoo-whoo'.

'Now there's an unselfish mother for you!' said Grandfather. 'It's obvious she'd like them to have a good home. And they're probably getting a bit too big for her to manage.'

So the two owlets became regular members of our household, and, strangely enough, were among the few pets that Grandmother took a liking to. She objected to all snakes, most monkeys, and some crows, but she took quite a fancy to the owls, and frequently fed them spaghetti. They seemed quite fond of spaghetti. In fact, the owls became so attached to Grandmother that they began to show affection towards anyone in a petticoat, including Aunt Mabel, who was terrified of them. She would run shrieking from the room every time one of the birds sidled up to her in a friendly manner.

Forgetful of the fact that Grandfather and I had reared them, the owls would sometimes swell their feathers and snap at anyone in trousers. To avoid displeasing them, Grandfather wore a petticoat at feeding time. This mild form of transvestism appeared to satisfy them. I compromised by wearing an apron.

In response to Grandmother's voice, the owlets would make sounds as gentle and soothing as the purring of a cat; but when wild owls were around, ours would rend the night with blood-curdling shrieks. Their nightly occupation was catching beetles, with which the kitchen-quarters were infested at the time. With their sharp eyes and powerful beaks, they were excellent pest destroyers.

The owls loved to sit and splash in a shallow dish, especially if cold water was poured over them from a jug at the same time. They would get thoroughly wet, jump out on to a perch, shake themselves, then return for a second splash and sometimes a third. During the day they dozed in large cages under the trees in the garden. They needed cages for protection against attacks from wild birds. At night they had the freedom of the house, where they exercised their wings as much as they liked. Superstitious folk, who dread the cry of the owl, may be interested to know that—mice excepted—there were no untoward deaths in the house during the owls' residence.

Looking back on those owlish days, I carry in my mind a picture of Grandmother with a contented look in her rocking-chair. Once, on entering her room while she was having an afternoon nap, I saw that one of the owls had crawled up her pillow till its head was snuggled under her ear. Both Grandmother and the little owl were snoring.

THE ELEPHANT AND THE CASSOWARY

The baby elephant wasn't out of place in our home in north India because India is where elephants belong, and in any case our house was full of pets brought home by Grandfather, who was in the Forest Service. But the cassowary bird was different. No one had ever seen such a bird before—not in India, at least. Grandfather had picked it up on a voyage to Singapore, where he'd been given the bird by a rubber planter who'd got it from a Dutch trader who'd got it from a man in Indonesia.

Anyway, it ended up at our home in Dehra, and seemed to do quite well in the subtropical climate. It looked like a cross between a turkey and an ostrich, but bigger than the former, and smaller than the latter—about five feet in height. It was not a beautiful bird, nor even a friendly one, but it had come to stay, and everyone was curious about it, especially the baby elephant.

Right from the start the baby elephant took a great interest in the cassowary, a bird unlike any found in the Indian jungles.

He would circle round the odd creature and diffidently examine with his trunk the texture of its stumpy wings; of course, he suspected no evil, and his childlike curiosity encouraged him to take liberties which resulted in an unpleasant experience.

Noticing the baby elephant's attempts to make friends with the rather morose cassowary, we felt a bit apprehensive. Self-contained and sullen, the big bird responded only by slowly and slyly raising one of its powerful legs, in the meantime gazing into space with an innocent air. We knew what the gesture meant; we had seen that treacherous leg raised on many an occasion, and suddenly shooting out with a force that would have done credit to a vicious camel. In fact, camel and cassowary kicks are delivered in the same way, except that the camel kicks backward like a horse and the bird forward.

We wished to spare our baby elephant a painful experience, and led him away from the bird. But he persisted in his friendly overtures, and one morning he received an ugly reward. Rapid as lightning, the cassowary hit straight from the hip and knee joints, and the elephant ran squealing to Grandmother.

For several days he avoided the cassowary, and we thought he had learnt his lesson. He crossed and recrossed the compound and the garden, swinging his trunk, thinking furiously. Then, about a week later, he appeared on the veranda at breakfast time in his usual cheery, childlike fashion, sidling up to the cassowary as if nothing had happened.

We were struck with amazement at this and so, it seemed, was the bird. Had the painful lesson already been forgotten, and by a member of the elephant tribe noted for its ability never to forget? Another dose of the same medicine would serve the baby right.

The cassowary once more began to draw up its fighting leg with sinister determination. It was nearing the true position for the master kick, kung fu style, when all of a sudden the baby elephant seized with his trunk the cassowary's other leg and pulled it down. There was a clumsy flapping of wings, a tremendous swelling of the bird's wattle, and an undignified getting up, as if it were a floored boxer doing his best to beat the count of ten. The bird then marched off with an attempt to look stately and unconcerned, while we at the breakfast table were convulsed with laughter.

After this the cassowary bird gave the baby elephant as wide a berth as possible. But they were not forced to coexist for very long. The baby elephant, getting bulky and cumbersome, was sold and now lives in a zoological garden where he is a favourite with young visitors who love to take rides on his back.

As for the cassowary, he continued to grace our veranda for many years, gaped at, but not made much of, while entering a rather friendless old age.

IN DEFENCE OF SNAKES

It is difficult to understand the reasons for people reacting in such a petrified way to the presence of a snake on the road, in the garden, or on the back veranda. After first freezing with fright, and then discovering that the snake has no evil intentions, humans become very brave indeed, shouting 'Snake, snake!' until other humans arrive, armed with stout sticks. And if by that time the snake has not made itself scarce, it is beaten to death.

I suppose it all has something to do with the story of the devil taking the form of a serpent in order to tempt Eve. But Eve would have fallen anyway, regardless of what earthly form the devil took.

Poor dead snake! All that it ever intended was to bask in the sun for a few minutes between showers, and, if possible, snap up a dallying frog. Instead it finds itself surrounded by a group of terrified and terrifying humans, all determined to put an end to its existence.

Most of the snakes that are killed in this way are perfectly harmless specimens. Of the 300 different species in India, there are only forty which may be considered dangerous, and of these there are just five which can kill a healthy, grown man. All snakes are poisonous, but some snakes are more poisonous than others. Most of them carry just enough venom to paralyse their natural prey, which consists of frogs, rats, birds, earthworms, and smaller snakes. Pythons don't need any venom. Once they have taken a firm grip on you, they simply squeeze away until all your bones are crushed; and then they start swallowing—preferably starting with the head. But pythons don't need more than two or three good meals in a year, so you are quite safe with a pet python provided you don't starve it.

But even a dangerous snake won't attack you unless it is trodden upon, or in some way provoked. One hears of thousands of people dying from snakebite every year. If this is true, then it is due more to human carelessness than to reptilian aggressiveness. I have yet to come across a victim of snakebite; and I have yet to come across a snake who showed the least inclination to bite me. (As compared to scorpions and centipedes, who can be quite vicious.) After all, snakes kill mainly in order to eat; and no snake that I know of (except, of course, the amiable python) is greedy enough, or large enough, to want to swallow me in my entirety.

My tolerance towards snakes has not gone unrewarded. I have noticed a significant reduction in the frog population. The operatic warbling that kept me awake at night has ceased, and I sleep in peace. I am even thinking of allowing the green snake into the house occasionally, to see if it will rid me of the field rats who have taken up residence for the duration of the monsoon. I have nothing to lose. My friends have already stopped coming to see me; but so have my creditors.

THE ADVENTURES OF TOTO

Grandfather bought Toto from a tonga driver for a sum of five rupees. The tonga driver used to keep the little red monkey tied to a feeding trough, and the monkey looked so out of place there that Grandfather decided he would add the little fellow to his private zoo.

Toto was a pretty monkey. His bright eyes sparkled with mischief beneath deep-set eyebrows, and his teeth, which were a pearly white, were very often displayed in a smile that frightened the life out of elderly Anglo-Indian ladies. But his hands looked dried up, as though they had been pickled in the sun for many years. Yet his fingers were quick and wicked; and his tail, while adding to his good looks (Grandfather believed a tail would add to anyone's good looks), also served as a third hand. He could use it to hang from a branch; and it was capable of scooping up any delicacy that might be out of reach of his hands.

Grandmother always fussed when Grandfather brought home some new bird or animal. So it was decided that Toto's presence should be kept a secret from her until she was in a particularly good mood. Grandfather and I put him away in a little closet opening into my bedroom wall, where he was tied securely—or so we thought—to a peg fastened into the wall.

A few hours later, when Grandfather and I came back to release Toto, we found that the walls, which had been covered with some ornamental paper chosen by Grandfather, now stood out as naked brick and plaster. The peg in the wall had been wrenched from its socket, and my school blazer, which had been hanging there, was in shreds. I wondered what Grandmother would say. But Grandfather didn't worry; he seemed pleased with Toto's performance.

'He's clever,' said Grandfather. 'Given time, I'm sure he could have tied the torn pieces of your blazer into a rope, and made his escape from the window!'

His presence in the house still a secret, Toto was now transferred to a big cage in the servants' quarters where a number of Grandfather's pets lived very sociably together—a tortoise, a pair of rabbits, a tame squirrel, and, for a while, my pet goat. But the monkey wouldn't allow any of his companions to sleep at night; so Grandfather, who had to leave Dehradun the next day to collect his pension in Saharanpur, decided to take him along.

Unfortunately, I could not accompany Grandfather on that trip, but he told me about it afterwards. A big black canvas kitbag was provided for Toto. This, with some straw at the bottom, became his new abode. When the strings of the bag were tied, there was no escape. Toto could not get his hands through the opening, and the canvas was too strong for him to bite his way through. His efforts to get out only had the effect of making the bag roll about on the floor or occasionally jump into the air—an exhibition that attracted a curious crowd of onlookers on the Dehradun railway platform.

Toto remained in the bag as far as Saharanpur, but while Grandfather was producing his ticket at the railway turnstile, Toto suddenly poked his head out of the bag and gave the ticket collector a wide grin.

The poor man was taken aback; but, with great presence of mind and much to Grandfather's annoyance, he said, 'Sir, you have a dog with you. You'll have to pay for it accordingly.'

In vain did Grandfather take Toto out of the bag; in vain did he try to prove that a monkey did not qualify as a dog, or even as a quadruped. Toto was classified a dog by the ticket collector; and three rupees was the sum handed over as his fare. Then Grandfather, just to get his own back, took from his pocket our pet tortoise, and said, 'What must I pay for this, since you charge for all animals?'

The ticket collector looked closely at the tortoise, prodded it with his forefinger, gave Grandfather a pleased and triumphant look, and said, 'No charge. It is not a dog.'

When Toto was finally accepted by Grandmother, he was given a comfortable home in the stable, where he had for a companion the family donkey, Nana. On Toto's first night in the stable, Grandfather paid him a visit to see if he was comfortable. To his surprise he found Nana, without apparent cause, pulling at her tether and trying to keep her head as far as possible from a bundle of hay.

Grandfather gave Nana a slap across her haunches,

and she jerked back, dragging Toto with her. He had fastened on to her long ears with his sharp little teeth.

Toto and Nana never became friends.

A great treat for Toto during cold winter evenings was the large bowl of warm water given to him by Grandmother for his bath. He would cunningly test the temperature with his hand, then gradually step into the bath, first one foot, then the other (as he had seen me doing), until he was in the water up to his neck. Once comfortable, he would take the soap in his hands or feet, and rub himself all over. When the water became cold, he would get out, and run as quickly as he could to the kitchen fire in order to dry himself. If anyone laughed at him during this performance, Toto's feelings would be hurt and he would refuse to go on with his bath.

One day Toto nearly succeeded in boiling himself alive.

A large kitchen kettle had been left on the fire to boil for tea. And Toto, finding himself with nothing better to do, decided to remove the lid. Finding the water just warm enough for a bath, he got in, with his head sticking out from the open kettle. This was just fine for a while, until the water began to boil. Toto then raised himself a little; but, finding it cold outside, sat down again. He continued hopping up and down for some time, until Grandmother arrived and hauled him, half-boiled, out of the kettle.

If there is a part of the brain especially devoted to mischief, that part was largely developed in Toto. He was always tearing things to pieces. Whenever one of my aunts came near him, he made every effort to get hold of her dress and tear a hole in it.

One day, at lunchtime, a large dish of pulao rice stood in the centre of the dining table. We entered the room to find Toto stuffing himself with rice. My grandmother screamed—and Toto threw a plate at her. One of my aunts rushed forward and received a glass of water in the face. When Grandfather arrived, Toto picked up the dish of pulao and made his exit through a window. We found him in the branches of the jackfruit tree, the dish still in his arms. He remained there all afternoon, eating slowly through the rice, determined on finishing every grain. And then, in order to spite Grandmother, who had screamed at him, he threw the dish down from the tree, and chattered with delight when it broke into a hundred pieces.

Obviously Toto was not the sort of pet we could keep for long. Even Grandfather realized that. We were not well-to-do, and could not afford the frequent loss of dishes, clothes, curtains, and wallpaper. So Grandfather found the tonga driver, and sold Toto back to him—for only three rupees.

THE CONCEITED PYTHON

There was one pet which Grandfather could not keep for very long. Grandmother was tolerant of some birds and animals, but she drew the line at reptiles. Even a chameleon as sweet-tempered as Henry (we will come to him later) made her blood run cold. Grandfather should have known that there was little chance of being allowed to keep a python.

He never could resist buying unusual pets, and while we still had Toto, he paid a snake charmer in the bazaar only four rupees for the young four-foot python that was on display to a crowd of eager boys and girls. Grandfather impressed the gathering by slinging the python over his shoulders and walking home with it.

The first to see them arrive was Toto, swinging from a branch of the jackfruit tree. One look at the python, ancient enemy of his race, and he fled into the house, squealing with fright. The noise brought Grandmother on to the veranda, where she nearly fainted at the sight of the python curled around Grandfather's neck.

'It will strangle you to death,' she cried. 'Get rid of it at once!'

'Nonsense!' said Grandfather. 'He's only a young fellow—he'll soon get used to us.'

'He might, indeed,' said Grandmother, 'but I have no intention of getting used to him. And you know your cousin Mabel is coming to stay with us tomorrow. She'll leave the minute she knows there's a snake in the house.'

'Well, perhaps we should show it to her as soon as she arrives,' said Grandfather, who did not look forward to the visits of relatives any more than I did.

'You'll do no such thing,' said Grandmother.

'Well, I can't let it loose in the garden. It might find its way into the poultry house and then where would we be?'

'Oh, how irritating you are!' grumbled Grandmother. 'Lock the thing in the bathroom, then go out and find the man you bought it from, and get him to come here and collect it.'

And so, in my awestruck presence, Grandfather took the python into the bathroom and placed it in the tub. After closing the door on it, he gave me a sad look. 'Perhaps Grandmother is right this time,' he said. 'After all, we don't want the snake to get hold of Toto. And it's sure to be very hungry.'

He hurried off to the bazaar to look for the snake charmer, and was gone for about two hours, while Grandmother paced up and down the veranda. When Grandfather returned, looking crestfallen, we knew he had not been able to find the snake charmer.

'Well, then, kindly take it away yourself,' said Grandmother. 'Leave it in the jungle across the riverbed.'

'All right, but let me feed it first,' said Grandfather. He produced a plucked chicken (in those days you could get a chicken for less than a rupee), and went into the bathroom, followed, in single file, by myself, Grandmother, and the cook and gardener.

Grandfather opened the door and stepped into the room. I peeped around his legs, while the others stayed well behind. We could not see the python anywhere.

'He's gone,' announced Grandfather.

'He couldn't have gone far,' said Grandmother. 'Look under the tub.'

We looked under the tub, but the python was not there. Then Grandfather went to the window. 'We left it open,' he said. 'He must have gone this way.'

A careful search was made of the house, the kitchen, the garden, the stable, and the poultry shed; but the python could not be found anywhere.

'He must have gone over the garden wall,' said Grandfather. 'He'll be well away by now.'

'I certainly hope so,' said Grandmother, with a look of relief.

Aunt Mabel arrived the next day for a three-week visit and for a couple of days Grandfather and I were a little worried in case the python made a sudden appearance; but on the third day, when he did not show up, we felt sure that he had gone for good.

And then, towards evening, we were startled by a scream from the garden. Seconds later Aunt Mabel came flying up the veranda steps, looking as though she had seen the devil himself.

'In the guava tree!' she gasped. 'I was reaching for a guava when I saw it staring at me. The look in its eyes! As though it would eat me alive....'

'Calm down, my dear,' urged Grandmother, sprinkling eau de cologne over my aunt. 'Tell us, what did you see?'

'A snake!' sobbed Aunt Mabel. 'A great boa constrictor. It must have been twenty feet long! In the guava tree. Its eyes were terrible. And it looked at me in such a queer way....'

My grandparents exchanged glances and Grandfather said, 'I'll go out and kill it.' Taking hold of an umbrella, he sallied forth into the garden. But when he got to the guava tree, the python had gone.

'Aunt Mabel must have frightened it away,' I said.

'Hush,' said Grandfather. 'We mustn't speak of your aunt in that way.' But his eyes were alive with laughter.

After this incident, the python began to make a number of appearances, always in the most unexpected places. Aunt Mabel had another fit when she saw him emerge from beneath a cushion. She packed her bags and left.

The hunt continued.

One morning I saw the python curled up on the dressing table, gazing at his own reflection in the mirror. I went for Grandfather, but by the time we returned to the room the python had moved on. He was seen in the garden and once the cook saw him crawling up the iron ladder to the roof. Then we found him on the dressing table a second time, admiring himself in the mirror. Evidently he was fascinated by his own reflection.

'All the attention he's getting has probably made him conceited,' said Grandfather.

'He's trying to look better for Aunt Mabel,' I said. (I regretted this remark because Grandmother overheard and held up my pocket money for the rest of the week.)

'Anyway, now we know his weakness,' said Grandfather.

'Are *you* trying to be funny too?' said Grandmother.

'I didn't mean Aunt Mabel,' explained Grandfather. 'The python is becoming vain, so it should be easier to catch him.'

Grandfather set about preparing a large cage, with a mirror at one end. In the cage he left a juicy chicken and several other tasty things. The opening was fitted up with a trapdoor.

Aunt Mabel had already left by the time we set up the trap, but we had to go on with the project because we could not have the python prowling about the house indefinitely. A python's bite is not poisonous, but it can swallow a live monkey, and it can be a risky playmate for a small boy.

For a few days nothing happened; and then, as I was leaving for school one morning, I saw the python in the cage. He had eaten everything left out for him, and was curled in front of the mirror, with something that resembled a smile on his face—if you can imagine a python smiling.

I lowered the trapdoor gently, but the python took no notice of me. Grandfather and the gardener put the cage in a tonga and took it across the riverbed. Opening the trapdoor, they left the cage in the jungle. When they went away, the python had made no attempt to get out.

'I didn't have the heart to take the mirror away from him,' said Grandfather. 'It's the first time I've seen a snake fall in love.'

A HORNBILL CALLED HAROLD

Harold's mother, like all good hornbills, was the most careful of wives; his father, the most easy-going of husbands. In January before the dhak tree burst into flame-red blossom, Harold's father took his wife into a giant hole high in the tree trunk, where his father and father's father had taken their brides at the same time every year. In this weather-beaten hollow, generation upon generation of hornbills had been raised; and Harold's mother, like those before her, was enclosed within the hole by a sturdy wall of earth, sticks, and dung.

Harold's father left a small slit in the centre of this wall, to enable him to communicate with his wife whenever he felt like a chat. Walled up in her uncomfortable room, Harold's mother was a prisoner for over two months. During this period an egg was laid, and Harold was born.

In his naked boyhood Harold was no beauty. His most prominent feature was his flaming red bill, matching the blossoms of the flame tree which were now ablaze, heralding the summer. He had a stomach that could never be filled, despite the best efforts of his parents, who brought him pieces of jackfruit and berries from the banyan tree.

As he grew bigger, the room became more cramped and one day his mother burst through the wall, spread out her wings, and sailed over the treetops. Her husband pretended he was glad to see her about and played with her, expressing his delight with deep gurgles and throaty chuckles. Then they repaired the wall of the nursery, so that Harold would not fall out.

Harold was quite happy in his cell, and felt no urge for freedom. He was putting on weight and feathers and acquiring a philosophy of his own. Then something happened to change the course of his life.

One afternoon he was awakened from his siesta by a loud banging on the wall, a banging quite different from that made by his parents. Soon the wall gave way, and there was something large and red staring at him—not his parents' bills, but Grandfather's sunburnt face and short red beard.

In a moment Harold was seized. He roared lustily and struck out with his bill and feet, but to no purpose. Grandfather had him in a bag, and the young hornbill was added to the zoo on our front veranda.

Harold had a simple outlook and once he had got over some early attacks of nerves, he began to welcome the approach of strangers. For him, Grandfather and I meant the arrival of food, and he greeted us with craning neck, quivering open bill, and a loud, croaking '*Ka-Ka-Kaee!*' Grandfather gave him a very roomy cage in a sunny corner of the veranda—a palace compared to the cramped quarters he had grown up in—and a basin of fresh water every day for his bath.

Harold was not beautiful by Indian standards. He had a small body and a large head. But his nature was friendly and he stayed on good terms with both my grandparents during his twelve years as a member of the household. He would even tolerate my aunts, to whom most of the other pets in the house usually took a strong dislike.

Harold's best friends were those who fed him, and he was even willing to share his food with us, sometimes trying to feed me with his great beak. Eating was a serious business for Harold, and if there was any delay at mealtimes he would summon us with raucous barks and vigorous bangs of his bill on the woodwork of his cage.

He loved bananas and dates and balls of boiled rice. I would throw him the rice-balls, and he would catch them in his beak, toss them into the air, and let them drop into his open mouth. He perfected his trick of catching things and Grandfather trained him to catch a tennis ball thrown with some force from a distance of fifteen yards. Harold would have made an excellent slip fielder at cricket.

Having no family, profession, or religion, Harold gave much time and thought to his personal appearance. He carried a rouge-pot on his person and used it very skilfully as an item of his morning toilet. This rouge-pot was a small gland situated above the roots of his tail feathers; it produced a rich yellow fluid. Harold would dip into his rouge-pot from time to time and then rub the colour over his feathers and the back of his neck. The colour came off on one's hands when one touched Harold. I think his colour had some sort of waterproofing effect because he used his colour-pot most during the rains.

Harold never drank anything, not even water, in all the years he stayed with Grandfather. Apparently hornbills get all the liquid they need from their solid food.

Only once did he misbehave. That was when he removed a lighted cigar from the hand of an American friend who was visiting us and swallowed it. It was a moving experience for Harold and an unnerving one for our guest. Both had to be given some brandy.

Though Harold drank no water, he loved the rain. We always knew when it was going to rain, because Harold would start chuckling to himself about one hour before the raindrops fell. This used to irritate my aunts. They were always being caught in the rain. Harold would be chuckling when they left the house; and when they returned drenched to the skin, he would be in fits of laughter.

As the storm clouds gathered, and gusts of wind shook the banana trees, Harold would get very excited, and his chuckle would change to an eerie whistle. '*Wheee...wheee*' he would scream. And then, as the first drops of rain hit the veranda steps, and the scent of the freshened earth passed through the house, he would start roaring again like a drunk. The wind would sweep the rain into his spacious cage, and Harold would spread out his wings and dance, tumbling about like a circus clown.

When the monsoon really set in, he would get used

to the rains, and his enthusiasm, like our own, would lessen. But the first few showers were always a wonder to him and we would come out on the veranda to watch him and share in his pleasure.

I miss Harold's raucous bark, and the banging of his great bill. If there is a heaven for good hornbills, I hope he is getting all the summer showers he could wish for and plenty of tennis balls to catch.

A LITTLE WORLD OF MUD

I had never thought there was much to be found in the rainwater pond behind our house except for quantities of mud and the occasional water buffalo. It was Grandfather who introduced me to the pond's diversity of life, so beautifully arranged that each individual gained some benefit from the well-being of the mass. To the inhabitants of the pond, the pond was the world; and to the inhabitants of the world, commented Grandfather, the world was but a muddy pond.

When Grandfather first showed me the pond world, he chose a dry place in the shade of an old peepul tree, where we sat for an hour, gazing steadily at the thin green scum on the water. The buffaloes had not arrived for their afternoon dip, the surface of the pond was undisturbed.

For the first ten minutes we saw nothing. Then a small black blob appeared in the middle of the pond. Gradually it rose higher until at last we could make out a frog's head, its big eyes staring hard at us. He did not know if we were friend or enemy and kept his body out of sight. A heron, his mortal enemy, might have been wading about in search of him. When he had made sure that we were not herons, he passed this information to his friends and neighbours, and very soon there were a number of big heads and eyes on the surface of the water. Throats swelled, and there began a chorus which went, '*wurk, wurk, wurk...*'.

In the shallow water near the tree we could see a dark, shifting shadow. When we touched it with the end of a stick, the dark mass immediately became alive. Thousands of little black tadpoles wriggled into life, pushing and hustling one another.

'What do tadpoles eat?' I asked Grandfather.

'They eat one another much of the time,' said Grandfather, who had once kept a few in an aquarium. 'It may seem an unpleasant custom, but when you think of the thousands of tadpoles that are hatched, you will realize what a useful system it is. If all the young tadpoles in this pond became frogs, they would take up every inch of ground between us and the house!'

'Their croaking would certainly drive Grandmother crazy,' I said, to which Grandfather agreed.

When Grandfather was younger, he had once brought home a number of green tree frogs. He put them in a glass jar and left them on a windowsill without telling anyone, anyone at all, of their presence.

At about four in the morning the entire household was awakened by a loud and fearful noise, and Grandmother and several nervous relatives gathered on the veranda for safety. Their fear turned to anger when they discovered the source of the noise. At the first glimmer of dawn, the frogs had with one accord burst into song. Grandmother wanted to throw the frogs, bottle and all, out of the window, but Grandfather gave the bottle a good shaking, and the frogs stayed quiet. Everyone went to sleep again but Grandfather was obliged to stay awake in order to shake the bottle whenever the frogs showed signs of bursting into song again.

Fortunately for all concerned, the next day Aunt Mabel took the top off the bottle to see what was inside. The sight of a dozen green tree frogs so frightened her that she ran off without replacing the cover, and the frogs jumped out and got loose in the garden and were never seen again.

Their escape ruined Grandfather's project of using the tree frogs as barometers. His idea was to place the frogs in tall bottles with wooden ladders. The steps of the ladder would act as degree-marks. The frogs would climb to the top in fine weather but keep to the bottom of the bottle in bad weather. It was Grandfather's plan to consult his frogs before going out on picnics.

But to return to my own pond....

I soon grew into the habit of visiting it on my own, to explore its banks and shallows; and, taking off my shoes, I would wade into the muddy water up to my knees and pluck the water lilies off the surface.

One day, when I reached the pond, I found it already occupied by the buffaloes. Their owner, a boy a little older than I, was swimming about in the middle of the pond. Instead of climbing out on to the bank, he would pull himself up on the back of one of his buffaloes, stretch his naked brown body out on the animal's glistening back, and start singing to himself.

When the boy saw me staring at him from across the pond, he smiled, showing gleaming white teeth in his dark, sunburnt face. He invited me to join him in a swim. I told him I could not swim and he offered to teach me. He dived off the back of his buffalo and swam across to me. And I, having removed my shirt and shorts, followed his instructions until I was struggling about among the water lilies.

The boy's name was Ramu, and he promised to give me swimming lessons every afternoon. And so it was during the afternoons—especially summer afternoons when everyone else was asleep—that we met.

Very soon I was able to swim across the pond to sit with Ramu astride a contented buffalo, standing like an island in the middle of a muddy ocean. Ramu came from a family of farmers and had as yet received no schooling. But he was well-versed in folklore and knew a great deal about birds and animals,

I liked the buffaloes too. Sometimes we would try racing them, Ramu and I riding on different buffaloes. But they were lazy creatures, and would leave one comfortable spot only for another or, if they were in no mood for games, would roll over on their backs, taking us with them into the mud and green scum of the pond. I would often emerge from the pond in shades of green and khaki, then slip into the house through the bathroom, bathing under the tap before getting into my clothes.

Ramu and I sat on our favourite buffalo and watched a pair of sarus cranes prancing and capering around each other: tall, stork-like birds with naked red heads and long red legs. They are always very devoted companions, and it is said that if a sarus is killed its mate will haunt the scene for weeks, calling sadly, and sometimes pining away and dying of grief. They are held in great affection by village people, and when caught young, make excellent pets. Though Grandfather did not keep a sarus crane, he said they were as good as watchdogs, giving loud trumpet-like calls when they were disturbed.

'Many birds are sacred,' said Ramu, as a blue jay swooped down from the peepul tree and carried off a grasshopper. He told me that both the blue jay and Lord Shiva were called Nilkanth. Shiva had a blue throat, like the bird, because out of compassion for the human race, he had swallowed a deadly poison meant to destroy the world. Keeping the poison in his throat, he did not let it go down any further.

'Are squirrels sacred?' I asked.

'Lord Rama loved squirrels,' said Ramu. 'He would take them in his arms and stroke them with his long fingers. That is why they have four dark lines down their backs from head to tail. The lines are the marks of his fingers.'

It seemed that both Ramu and Grandfather were of the opinion that we should be more gentle with birds and animals, and not kill so many of them.

'It is also important that we respect them,' said Grandfather. 'We must acknowledge their rights on the earth. Everywhere, birds and animals are finding it more difficult to live because we are destroying their forests.

They have to keep moving as the trees disappear.'

Ramu and I spent many long summer afternoons at the pond. Only the buffaloes and the frogs and the sarus cranes knew of our friendship. They had accepted us as part of their own world, their muddy but comfortable pond. And when finally I went away, both they and Ramu must have assumed that I would return like the birds.

THE BANYAN TREE

Though the house and grounds belonged to my
grandparents, the magnificent old banyan tree was
mine—chiefly because Grandfather, at sixty-five, could
no longer climb it.

Its spreading branches, which hung to the ground and
took root again, forming a number of twisting passages,
gave me endless pleasure. Among them were squirrels
and snails and butterflies. The tree was older than the
house, older than Grandfather, as old as Dehradun itself.
I could hide myself in its branches, behind thick green
leaves, and spy on the world below.

My first friend was a small grey squirrel. Arching
his back and sniffing into the air, he seemed at first to
resent my invasion of his privacy. But when he found
that I did not arm myself with catapult or airgun, he
became friendly, and when I started bringing him pieces
of cake and biscuit, he grew quite bold and was soon
taking morsels from my hand.

Before long he was delving into my pockets and
helping himself to whatever he could find. He was a
very young squirrel and his friends and relatives probably
thought him foolish and headstrong for trusting a human.

In the spring, when the banyan tree was full of small

red figs, birds of all kinds would flock into its branches: the red-bottomed bulbul, cheerful and greedy; gossipy rosy pastors; parrots, mynas, and crows squabbling with one another. During the fig season, the banyan tree was the noisiest place in the garden.

Halfway up the tree I had built a crude platform where I would spend the afternoons when it was not too hot. I could read there, propping myself up against the bole of the tree with a cushion from the living room. *Treasure Island*, *The Adventures of Huckleberry Finn*, and *The Story of Doctor Dolittle* were some of the books that made up my banyan tree library.

When I did not feel like reading, I could look down through the leaves at the world below. And, on one particular afternoon, I had a grandstand view of that classic of the Indian wilds, a fight between a mongoose and a cobra. And this one had been staged for my benefit!

The warm breezes of approaching summer had sent everyone, including the gardener, into the house. I was feeling drowsy myself, wondering if I should go to the pond and have a swim with Ramu and the buffaloes, when I saw a huge black cobra gliding out of a clump of cactus. At the same time a mongoose emerged from the bushes and went straight for the cobra.

In a clearing beneath the banyan tree, in bright sunshine, they came face to face.

The cobra knew only too well that the grey mongoose, three feet long, was a superb fighter, clever and aggressive. But the cobra, too, was a skilful and experienced fighter. He could move swiftly and strike with the speed of light;

and the sacs behind his long, sharp fangs were full of deadly poison.

It was to be a battle of champions.

Hissing defiance, his forked tongue darting in and out, the cobra raised three of his six feet off the ground and spread his spectacled hood. The mongoose bushed his tail. The long hair on his spine stood up.

Though the combatants were unaware of my presence in the tree, they were soon made aware of the arrival of two other spectators. One was a myna, the other a jungle crow. They had seen these preparations for battle and had settled on the cactus to watch the outcome. Had they been content only to watch, all would have been well with both of them.

The cobra stood on the defensive, swaying slowly from side to side, trying to mesmerize the mongoose into making a false move. But the mongoose knew the power of his opponent's glassy, unwinking eyes, and refused to meet them. Instead, he fixed his gaze at a point just below the cobra's hood and opened the attack.

Moving forward quickly, until he was just within the cobra's reach, the mongoose made a pretended move to one side. Immediately the cobra struck. His great hood came down so swiftly that I thought nothing could save the mongoose. But the little fellow jumped neatly to one side, and darted in as swiftly as the cobra, biting the snake on the back and darting away again out of reach.

At the same moment that the cobra struck, the crow and the myna hurled themselves at him, only to collide heavily in mid-air. Shrieking insults at each other, they returned to the cactus plant.

A few drops of blood glistened on the cobra's back. The cobra struck again and missed. Again the mongoose sprang aside, jumped in and bit. Again, the birds dived at the snake, bumped into each other instead and returned shrieking to the safety of the cactus.

The third round followed the same course as the first two with one dramatic difference. The crow and the myna, determined to take part in the proceedings, dived at the snake but this time they missed each other as well as their mark. The myna flew on and reached its perch, but the crow tried to pull up in mid-air and turn back. In the second that it took the bird to do this, the cobra whipped his head back and struck with great force, his snout thudding against the crow's body.

I saw the bird flung nearly twenty feet across the garden. It fluttered about for a while, then lay still. The myna remained on the cactus plant, and when the snake and the mongoose returned to the fight, very wisely decided not to interfere again!

The cobra was weakening, and the mongoose, walking fearlessly up to it, raised himself on his short legs and with a lightning snap had the big snake by the snout. The cobra writhed and lashed about in a frightening manner, and even coiled itself about the mongoose, but to no avail. The little fellow hung grimly on, until the snake had ceased to struggle. He then smelt it along its quivering length, gripped it round the hood, and dragged it into the bushes.

The myna dropped cautiously to the ground, hopped

about, jeered into the bushes from a safe distance, and then, with a shrill cry of congratulation, flew away.

The banyan tree was also the setting for what we were to call the Strange Case of the Grey Squirrel and the White Rat.

The white rat was Grandfather's—he had bought it for one-quarter of a rupee but I would often take it with me into the banyan tree, where it soon struck up a friendship with one of the squirrels. They would go off together on little excursions among the roots and branches of the old tree.

Then the squirrel started building a nest. At first she tried building it in my pockets, and when I went indoors and took off my clothes I would find straw and grass falling out.

Then one day Grandmother's knitting was missing. We hunted for it everywhere but without success.

The next day I saw something glinting in a hole in the tree. Going up to investigate, I saw that it was the end of Grandmother's steel knitting needle. On looking further, I discovered that the hole was crammed with knitting. Amongst the wool were three baby squirrels— and all of them were white!

We gazed at the white squirrels in wonder and fascination. Grandfather was puzzled at first, but when I told him about the white rat's visits to the tree, his brow cleared. He said the white rat must be the father.

HENRY: A CHAMELEON

This is the story of Henry, our pet chameleon. Chameleons are in a class by themselves and are no ordinary reptiles. From their nearest relatives, the lizards, they are easily distinguished by certain outstanding marks. Henry's tongue was as long as his body. On his head was a rigid crest which looked like a fireman's helmet. His limbs were long and slender and his fingers and toes were more developed than those of other reptiles.

Henry's most remarkable characteristics were his eyes. They were not beautiful. But his left eye was quite independent of his right. He could move one eye without disturbing the other. This gave him a horrible squint. Each eyeball, raised out of his head, wobbled up and down, backwards and forwards, quite independently of its partner. Reptiles are not gifted like us with binocular vision. They do not see an object with both eyes at once.

Whenever I visited Henry, he would treat me with great caution, sitting perfectly still on his perch with his back to me, but his nearest eye would move around like the beam of a searchlight until it had got me well in focus. Then it would stop and the other eye would proceed to carry out an independent survey of its own in some different direction. Henry took nobody on trust, and treated my friendliest gestures with grave suspicion.

Tiring of his attitude, I would tickle him gently in the ribs with my finger. This always threw him into a great rage. He would blow himself up to an enormous size, his lungs filling his body with air. He would sit up on his hind legs, swaying from side to side, hoping to overawe me. Opening his mouth very wide, he would let out an angry hiss. But his protests went no further. He did not bite. Non-violence was his creed.

Many people believe the chameleon is a dangerous and poisonous reptile. When Grandfather was visiting a friend in the country, he came upon a noisy scene at the garden gate. Men were shouting, hurling stones, and brandishing sticks. The cause of all this was a chameleon who had been discovered sunning himself on a shrub. The gardener declared that it was a thing capable of poisoning people at a distance of twenty feet, and as a result the entire household had risen up in arms. Grandfather was in time to save the chameleon from certain death, and brought the little reptile home.

That chameleon was Henry and that was how he came to live with us.

Henry was a harmless creature. If I put my finger in his mouth, even in his wildest moments, he would simply wait for me to take it out again. I suppose he could bite. His rigid jaws carried a number of fine, pointed teeth. But Henry was rightly convinced that these were given to him solely for the purpose of chewing his food.

Provided I was patient, Henry was willing to take food from my hands. This he did very swiftly. His tongue was a sort of boomerang which came back to him with the food, an insect victim, attached to it. Before I could realize what had happened, the grasshopper held between my fingers would be lodged between Henry's jaws.

Henry did not cause any trouble in our house, but he did create something like a riot in the nursery school down the road.

It happened like this.

When the papayas in our garden were ripe, Grandmother usually sent a basket of them to her friend, Mrs Ghosh, who was the principal of the nursery school. On this occasion, Henry managed to smuggle himself into the basket of papayas when no one was looking. (He did have a cage of his own, but was seldom in it.) The gardener dutifully carried the papayas across to the school and left them in Mrs Ghosh's office. When Mrs Ghosh came in after making her rounds, she began admiring and examining the papayas. Out popped Henry.

Mrs Ghosh screamed. Henry would probably have liked to blush a deep red, but he turned a bright green instead, as that was the colour of the papayas. Mrs. Ghosh's assistant, Miss Daniels, rushed in, took one look at the chameleon, and joined in the screaming. Henry took fright and fled from the office, running down the corridor and into one of the classrooms. There he climbed on to a desk, while children ran in all directions, some to get away from Henry, some to catch him. But Henry made his exit from a window and disappeared in the garden.

Grandmother heard all about the incident from Mrs Ghosh but did not tell her the chameleon was ours. I did not think Henry would find his way back to us, because the school was three houses away. But three days later, I found him sunning himself on the garden wall. He readily accepted some food from my hand and allowed himself to be recaptured.

UNCLE KEN'S RUMBLE IN THE JUNGLE

Uncle Ken drove Grandfather's old Fiat along the forest road at an incredible 30 mph, scattering pheasants, partridges, and jungle fowl as he went along. He had come in search of the disappearing red jungle fowl, and I could see why the bird had disappeared. Too many noisy human beings had invaded its habitat.

By the time we reached the forest rest house, one of the car doors had fallen off its hinges, and a large lantana bush had got entwined in the bumper.

'Never mind,' said Uncle Ken. 'It's all part of the adventure.'

The rest house had been reserved for Uncle Ken, thanks to Grandfather's good relations with the forest department. But I was the only other person in the car. No one else would trust himself or herself to Uncle Ken's driving. He treated a car as though it were a low-flying aircraft having some difficulty in getting off the runway.

As we arrived at the rest house, a number of hens made a dash for safety.

'Look, jungle fowl!' exclaimed Uncle Ken.

'Domestic fowl,' I said. 'They must belong to the forest guards.'

I was right, of course. One of the hens was destined

to be served up as chicken curry later that day. The jungle birds avoided the neighbourhood of the rest house, just in case they were mistaken for poultry and went into the cooking pot.

Uncle Ken was all for starting his search right away, and after a brief interval during which we were served tea and pakoras (prepared by the forest guard, who, it turned out, was also a good cook), we set off on foot into the jungle in search of the elusive red jungle fowl.

'No tigers around here, are there?' asked Uncle Ken, just to be on the safe side.

'No tigers on this range,' said the guard. 'Just elephants.'

Uncle Ken wasn't afraid of elephants. He'd been on numerous elephant rides at the Lucknow zoo. He'd also seen Sabu in *Elephant Boy*.

A small wooden bridge took us across a little river, and then we were in the jungle, following the forest guard who led us along a path that was frequently blocked by broken tree branches and pieces of bamboo.

'Why all these broken branches?' asked Uncle Ken.

'The elephants, sir,' replied our guard. 'They passed through last night. They like certain leaves, as well as young bamboo shoots.'

We saw a number of spotted deer and several pheasants, but no red jungle fowl.

That evening, we sat out on the veranda of the rest house. All was silent except for the distant trumpeting of elephants. Then, from the stream, came the chanting of hundreds of frogs.

There were tenors and baritones, sopranos and contraltos, and occasionally a bass deep enough to have pleased the great Chaliapin. They sang duets and quartets from *La Bohème* and other Italian operas, drowning out all other jungle sounds except for the occasional cry of a jackal doing his best to join in.

'We might as well sing too,' said Uncle Ken, and began singing 'Indian Love Call' in his best Nelson Eddy manner.

The frogs fell silent, obviously awestruck; but instead of receiving an answering love call, Uncle Ken was answered by even more strident jackal calls—not one, but several—with the result that all self-respecting denizens of the forest fled from the vicinity, and we saw no wildlife that night apart from a frightened rabbit that sped across the clearing and vanished into the darkness.

Early next morning, we renewed our efforts to track down the red jungle fowl, but it remained elusive. Returning to the rest house dusty and weary, Uncle Ken exclaimed: 'There it is—a red jungle fowl.'

But it turned out to be the caretaker's cock bird, a handsome fellow all red and gold, but not the jungle variety.

Disappointed, Uncle Ken decided to return to civilization. Another night in the rest house did not appeal to him. He had run out of songs to sing.

In any case, the weather had changed overnight and a light drizzle was falling as we started out. This had turned to a steady downpour by the time we reached the bridge across the Suswa River. And standing in the middle of the bridge was an elephant.

He was a long tusker and he didn't look too friendly. Uncle Ken blew his horn, and that was a mistake.

It was a strident, penetrating horn, highly effective on city roads but out of place in the forest.

The elephant took it as a challenge, and returned the blast of the horn with a shrill trumpeting of its own. It took a few steps forward. Uncle Ken put the car into reverse.

'Is there another way out of here?' he asked.

'There's a side road,' I said, recalling an earlier trip with Grandfather. 'It will take us to the Kansrao railway station.'

'What, ho!' cried Uncle Ken. 'To the station we go!'

And he turned the car and drove back until we came to the turning.

The narrow road was now a rushing torrent of rainwater and all of Uncle Ken's driving skills were put to the test. He had on one occasion driven through a brick wall, so he knew all about obstacles; but they were usually stationary ones.

'More elephants,' I said, as two large pachyderms loomed out of the rain-drenched forest.

'Elephants to the right of us, elephants to the left of us!' chanted Uncle Ken, misquoting Tennyson's 'Charge of the Light Brigade'. 'Into the valley of death rode the six hundred!'

'There are now three of them,' I observed.

'Not my lucky number,' said Uncle Ken and pressed hard on the accelerator. We lurched forward, almost running over a terrified barking deer.

'Is four your lucky number, Uncle Ken?'

'Why do you ask?'

'Well, there are now four of them behind us. And they are catching up quite fast!'

'I see the station ahead,' cried Uncle Ken, as we drove into a clearing where a tiny railway station stood like a beacon of safety in the wilderness.

The car came to a grinding halt. We abandoned it and ran for the building.

The stationmaster saw our predicament, and beckoned to us to enter the station building, which was little more than a two-room shed and platform. He took us inside his tiny control room and shut the steel gate behind us.

'The elephants won't bother you here,' he said. 'But say goodbye to your car.'

We looked out of the window and were horrified to see Grandfather's Fiat overturned by one of the elephants, while another proceeded to trample it underfoot. The other elephants joined in the mayhem and soon the car was a flattened piece of junk.

'I'm stationmaster Abdul Ranf,' the stationmaster introduced himself. 'I know a good scrap dealer in Doiwala. I'll give you his address.'

'But how do we get out of here?' asked Uncle Ken.

'Well, it's only an hour's walk to Doiwala, but not with those elephants around. Stay and have a cup of tea. The Dehra Express will pass through shortly. It stops for a few minutes. And it's only half an hour to Dehra from here.' He punched out a couple of rail tickets. 'Here you are, my friends. Just two rupees each. The cheapest rail journey in India. And these tickets carry an insurance value of two lakh rupees each, should an accident befall you between here and Dehradun.'

Uncle Ken's eyes lit up.

'You mean, if one of us falls out of the train?' he asked.

'Out of the moving train,' clarified the stationmaster. 'There will be an enquiry, of course, some people try to fake an accident.'

But Uncle Ken decided against falling out of the train and making a fortune. He'd had enough excitement for the day. We got home safely enough, taking a pony cart from Dehradun station to our house.

'Where's my car?' asked Grandfather, as we staggered up the veranda steps.

'It had a small accident,' said Uncle Ken. 'We left it outside the Kansrao railway station. I'll collect it later.'

'I'm starving,' I said. 'Haven't eaten since morning.'

'Well, come and have your dinner,' said Granny. 'I've made something special for you. One of your grandfather's hunting friends sent us a jungle fowl. I've made a nice roast. Try it with apple sauce.'

Uncle Ken did not ask if the jungle fowl was red, grey, or technicoloured. He was the first to the dining table.

Granny had anticipated this, and served me with a chicken leg, giving the other leg to Grandfather.

'I rather fancy the breast myself,' she said, and this left Uncle Ken with a long and scrawny neck—which was more than he deserved.

GRANDFATHER FIGHTS AN OSTRICH

Before my grandfather joined the Indian Railways, he worked for a few years on the East African Railways, and it was during that period that he had his now famous encounter with the ostrich. My childhood was frequently enlivened by this oft-told tale of his, and I give it here in his own words—or as well as I can remember them!

While engaged in the laying of a new railway line, I had a miraculous escape from an awful death. I lived in a small township, but my work lay some twelve miles away, and I had to go to the work site and back on horseback.

One day, my horse had a slight accident, so I decided to do the journey on foot, being a great walker in those days. I also knew of a shortcut through the hills that would save me about six miles.

This shortcut went through an ostrich farm—or 'camp', as it was called. It was the breeding season. I was fairly familiar with the ways of ostriches, and knew that male birds were very aggressive in the breeding season, ready to attack on the slightest provocation, but I also knew that my dog would scare away any bird that might try to attack me. Strange though it may seem, even the biggest ostrich (and some of them grow to a height of nine feet) will run faster than a racehorse at the sight of even a small dog. So, I felt quite safe in the company of my dog, a mongrel who had adopted me some two months previously.

On arrival at the camp, I climbed through the wire fencing and, keeping a good lookout, dodged across the open spaces between the thorn bushes. Now and then I caught a glimpse of the birds feeding some distance away.

I had gone about half a mile from the fencing when up started a hare. In an instant my dog gave chase. I tried calling him back, even though I knew it was hopeless. Chasing hares was that dog's passion.

I don't know whether it was the dog's bark or my own shouting, but what I was most anxious to avoid immediately happened. The ostriches were startled and began darting to and fro. Suddenly, I saw a big male bird emerge from a thicket about a hundred yards away. He stood still and stared at me for a few moments. I stared back. Then, expanding his short wings and with his tail erect, he came bounding towards me.

As I had nothing, not even a stick, with which to defend myself, I turned and ran towards the fence. But it was an unequal race. What were my steps of two or three feet against the creature's great strides of sixteen to twenty feet? There was only one hope: to get behind a large bush and try to elude the bird until help came. A dodging game was my only chance.

And so, I rushed for the nearest clump of thorn bushes and waited for my pursuer. The great bird wasted no time—he was immediately upon me.

Then the strangest encounter took place. I dodged this way and that, taking great care not to get directly in front of the ostrich's deadly kick. Ostriches kick forward, and with such terrific force that if you were struck, their huge, chisel-like nails would cause you much damage.

I was breathless, and really quite helpless, calling wildly for help as I circled the thorn bush. My strength was ebbing. How much longer could I keep going? I was ready to drop from exhaustion.

As if aware of my condition, the infuriated bird suddenly doubled back on his course and charged straight at me. With a desperate effort I managed to step to one side. I don't know how, but I found myself holding on to one of the creature's wings, quite close to its body.

It was now the ostrich's turn to be frightened. He began to turn, or rather waltz, moving round and round so quickly that my feet were soon swinging out from his body, almost horizontally! All the while the ostrich kept opening and shutting his beak with loud snaps.

Imagine my situation as I clung desperately to the wing of the enraged bird. He was whirling me round and round as though he were a discus-thrower—and I the discus! My arms soon began to ache with the strain, and the swift and continuous circling was making me dizzy. But I knew that if I relaxed my hold, even for a second, a terrible fate awaited me.

Round and round we went in a great circle. It seemed as if that spiteful bird would never tire. And, I knew I could not hold on much longer. Suddenly, the ostrich went into reverse! This unexpected move made me lose my hold and sent me sprawling to the ground. I landed in a heap near the thorn bush and, in an instant, before I even had time to realize what had happened, the big bird was upon me. I thought the end had come. Instinctively, I raised my hands to protect my face. But the ostrich did not strike.

I moved my hands from my face and there stood the creature with one foot raised, ready to deliver a deadly kick! I couldn't move. Was the bird going to play cat and mouse with me, and prolong the agony?

As I watched, frightened and fascinated, the ostrich turned his head sharply to the left. A second later he jumped back, turned, and made off as fast as he could go. Dazed, I wondered what had happened to make him beat so unexpected a retreat.

I soon found out. To my great joy, I heard the bark of my truant dog, and the next moment he was jumping around me, licking my face and hands. Needless to say, I returned his caresses most affectionately! And, I took good care to see that he did not leave my side until we were well clear of that ostrich camp.

A TIGER IN THE HOUSE

Timothy, the tiger cub, was discovered by Grandfather on a hunting expedition in the Terai jungle near Dehra.

Grandfather was no shikari, but as he knew the forests of the Siwalik hills better than most people, he was persuaded to accompany the party—it consisted of several Very Important Persons from Delhi—to advise on the terrain and the direction the beaters should take once a tiger had been spotted.

The camp itself was sumptuous—seven large tents (one for each shikari), a dining tent, and a number of servants' tents. The dinner was very good, as Grandfather admitted afterwards; it was not often that one saw hot-water plates, finger glasses, and seven or eight courses in a tent in the jungle! But that was how things were done in the days of the viceroys…. There were also some fifteen elephants, four of them with howdahs for the shikaris, and the others specially trained for taking part in the beat.

The sportsmen never saw a tiger, nor did they shoot anything else, though they saw a number of deer, peacock, and wild boar. They were giving up all hope of finding a tiger and were beginning to shoot at jackals when Grandfather, strolling down the forest path at some distance from the rest of the party, discovered a little tiger about eighteen inches long, hiding among the intricate roots of a banyan tree. Grandfather picked him up and brought him home after the camp had broken up. He had the distinction of being the only member of the party to have bagged any game, dead or alive.

At first the tiger cub, who was named Timothy by Grandmother, was brought up entirely on milk given to him in a feeding bottle by our cook, Mahmoud. But the milk proved too rich for him, and he was put on a diet of raw mutton and cod liver oil, to be followed later by a more tempting diet of pigeons and rabbits.

Timothy was provided with two companions—Toto the monkey, who was bold enough to pull the young tiger by the tail, and then climb up the curtains if Timothy lost his temper; and a small mongrel puppy, found on the road by Grandfather.

At first Timothy appeared to be quite afraid of the puppy and darted back with a spring if it came too near. He would make absurd dashes at it with his large forepaws and then retreat to a ridiculously safe distance. Finally, he allowed the puppy to crawl on his back and rest there!

One of Timothy's favourite amusements was to stalk anyone who would play with him, and so, when I came to live with Grandfather, I became one of the tiger's favourites. With a crafty look in his glittering eyes, and his body crouching, he would creep closer and closer to me, suddenly making a dash for my feet, rolling over on his back and kicking with delight, and pretending to bite my ankles.

He was by this time the size of a full-grown retriever, and when I took him out for walks, people on the road would give us a wide berth. When he pulled hard on his chain, I had difficulty in keeping up with him. His favourite place in the house was the drawing room, and he would make himself comfortable on the long sofa, reclining there with great dignity and snarling at anybody who tried to get him off.

Timothy had clean habits, and would scrub his face with his paws exactly like a cat. At night, he slept in the cook's quarters and was always delighted at being let out by him in the morning.

'One of these days,' declared Grandmother in her prophetic manner, 'we are going to find Timothy sitting on Mahmoud's bed, and no sign of the cook except his clothes and shoes!'

Of course, it never came to that, but when Timothy was about six months old a change came over him; he grew steadily less friendly. When out for a walk with me, he would try to steal away to stalk a cat or someone's pet Pekingese. Sometimes at night we would hear frenzied cackling from the poultry house, and in the morning there would be feathers lying all over the veranda. Timothy had to be chained up more often. And, finally, when he began to stalk Mahmoud about the house with what looked like villainous intent, Grandfather decided it was time to transfer him to a zoo.

The nearest zoo was at Lucknow, two hundred miles

away. Reserving a first-class compartment for himself and Timothy—no one would share a compartment with them—Grandfather took him to Lucknow where the zoo authorities were only too glad to receive as a gift a well-fed and fairly civilized tiger.

About six months later, when my grandparents were visiting relatives in Lucknow, Grandfather took the opportunity of calling at the zoo to see how Timothy was getting on. I was not there to accompany him, but I heard all about it when he returned to Dehra.

Arriving at the zoo, Grandfather made straight for the particular cage in which Timothy had been interned. The tiger was there, crouched in a corner, full-grown and with a magnificent striped coat.

'Hello, Timothy!' said Grandfather and, climbing the railing with ease, he put his arm through the bars of the cage.

The tiger approached the bars and allowed Grandfather to put both hands around his head. Grandfather stroked the tiger's forehead and tickled his ear, and, whenever he growled, smacked him across the mouth, which was his old way of keeping him quiet.

He licked Grandfather's hands and only sprang away when a leopard in the next cage snarled at him. Grandfather 'shooed' the leopard away and the tiger returned to lick his hands; but every now and then the leopard would rush at the bars and the tiger would slink back to his corner.

A number of people had gathered to watch the reunion when a keeper pushed his way through the crowd and asked Grandfather what he was doing.

'I'm talking to Timothy,' said Grandfather. 'Weren't you here when I gave him to the zoo six months ago?'

'I haven't been here very long,' said the surprised keeper. 'Please continue your conversation. But I have never been able to touch him myself, he is always very bad tempered.'

'Why don't you put him somewhere else?' suggested Grandfather. 'That leopard keeps frightening him. I'll go and see the superintendent about it.'

Grandfather went in search of the superintendent of the zoo, but found that he had gone home early; and so, after wandering about the zoo for a little while, he returned to Timothy's cage to say goodbye. It was beginning to get dark.

He had been stroking and slapping Timothy for about five minutes when he found another keeper observing him with some alarm. Grandfather recognized him as the keeper who had been there when Timothy had first come to the zoo.

'*You* remember me,' said Grandfather. 'Now why don't you transfer Timothy to another cage, away from this stupid leopard?'

'But—sir—' stammered the keeper, 'it is not your tiger.'

'I know, I know,' said Grandfather testily. 'I realize he is no longer mine. But you might at least take a suggestion or two from me.'

'I remember your tiger very well,' said the keeper. 'He died two months ago.'

'Died!' exclaimed Grandfather.

'Yes, sir, of pneumonia. This tiger was trapped in the hills only last month, and he is very dangerous!'

Grandfather could think of nothing to say. The tiger was still licking his arm, with increasing relish. Grandfather took what seemed to him an age to withdraw his hand from the cage.

With his face near the tiger's he mumbled, 'Goodnight, Timothy,' and giving the keeper a scornful look, walked briskly out of the zoo.

THE SONG OF THE WHISTLING THRUSH

In the wooded hills of western India lives 'The Idle Schoolboy'—a bird who cannot learn a simple tune, though he is gifted with one of the most beautiful voices in the forest. He whistles away in various sharps and flats, and sometimes, when you think he is really going to produce a melody, he breaks off in the middle of his song as though he has just remembered something very important.

Why is it that the whistling thrush can never remember a tune? The story goes that on a hot summer's afternoon, the young God Krishna was wandering along the banks of a mountain stream when he came to a small waterfall, shot through with sunbeams. It was a lovely spot, cool and inviting. Tiny fish flecked the pool at the foot of the waterfall, and a paradise flycatcher, trailing its silver tail, moved gracefully amongst the trees.

Krishna was enchanted. He threw himself down on a bed of moss and ferns, and began playing on his flute—the famous flute with which he had charmed all the creatures in the forest. A fat yellow lizard nodded its head in time to the music; the birds were hushed; and the shy mouse deer approached silently on their tiny hooves to see who it was who played so beautifully.

Presently the flute slipped from Krishna's fingers, and the beautiful young god fell asleep. But it was not a restful sleep, for his dreams were punctuated by an annoying whistling, as though someone who didn't know much about music was practising on his flute in an attempt to learn the tune that Krishna had been playing.

Awake now, Krishna sat up and saw a ragged urchin standing ankle-deep in the pool, the sacred flute held to his lips!

Krishna was furious.

'Come here, boy!' he shouted. 'How dare you steal my flute and disturb my sleep! Don't you know who I am?'

The boy, instead of being afraid, was thrilled at the discovery that he stood before his hero, the young Krishna, whose exploits were famous throughout the land.

'I did not steal your flute, lord,' he said. 'Had that been my intention, I would not have waited for you to wake up. It was only my great love for your music that made me touch your flute. You will teach me to play, will you not? I will be your disciple.'

Krishna's anger melted away, and he was filled with compassion for the boy. But it was too late to do anything, for it is everlastingly decreed that anyone who touches the sacred property of the gods, whether deliberately or in innocence, must be made to suffer throughout his next ten thousand births.

When this was explained to the boy, he fell on his face and wept bitterly, crying, 'Have mercy on me, Krishna.

Do with me as you will, but do not send me away from the beautiful forests I love.'

Swiftly, Krishna communed in spirit with Brahma the Creator. Here was a genuine case of a crime committed in ignorance. If it could not be forgiven, surely the punishment could be less severe?

Brahma agreed, and Krishna laid his hand on the boy's mouth, saying, 'For ever try to copy the song of the gods, but never succeed.' Then he touched the boy's clothes and said, 'Let the raggedness and dust disappear, and only the beautiful colours of Krishna remain.'

Immediately the boy was changed into the bird we know today as the whistling thrush of Malabar, with its dark body and brilliant blue patches on head and wings. In this guise, he still continues to live among the beautiful, forested valleys of the hills, where he tries unsuccessfully to remember the tune that brought about his strange transformation.

MONKEYS IN THE LOO

I am fairly tolerant about these monkeys doing the bhangra on my roof, but I do resent it when they start invading my rooms. Not so long ago, I opened the bathroom door to find a very large rhesus monkey sitting on the potty. He wasn't actually using the potty—monkeys prefer parapet walls—but he had obviously found it a comfortable place to sit, and he showed no signs of vacating the throne when politely requested to do so. Bullies seldom do. So I had to give him a fright by slamming the door as loudly as I could, and he took off through the open window and found his cousins on the hillside.

On another occasion, a female of the species sat on my desk, lifted the telephone receiver and appeared to be making an STD call to some distant relative. Some ladies are apt to linger long over their calls, and I hated to interrupt, but I was anxious to get in touch with my publisher, who took priority; so I pushed her off my desk with a feather duster. She was so resentful of this intrusion that she made off with my telephone directory and tore it to shreds, scattering pages along the road. As this was something that I had wanted to do for a long time, I could not help admiring her audacity.

The kitchen area of our flat is closely guarded, as I resent sharing my breakfast with creatures great and small. But the other day a wily crow flew in and made off with my boiled egg. I know crows are fond of eggs— other birds' eggs that is—but I did not know that they like them boiled. Anyway, this egg was still piping hot, and the crow had to drop it on the road, where it was seized upon by one of the stray dogs who police this end of the road.

Barking furiously, the dogs run after the monkeys, who simply leap on to the nearest tree or rooftop and proceed to throw insults at the frustrated pack. The dogs never succeed in catching anything except their own kind. Canine intruders from another area are readily attacked and driven away.

∽

Having dressed, breakfasted, and written the morning's two or three pages (early morning is the best time to do this), I am free to walk up the road to the bank or post office or tea shop at the top of the hill. If it's springtime, I shall look out for wild flowers. If it's monsoon time; I shall look out for leeches.

Well, it's monsoon time, and we haven't seen the sun for a couple of weeks. Clouds envelop the hills, and a light shower is falling. I have unfurled my bright yellow umbrella, as a gesture of defiance. At least it provides some contrast to the grey sky and the dark green of the hillside. You cannot see the snows or even the next mountain.

There's no one else on the road today, only a few intrepid tourists from Amritsar. I overheard one robust Punjabi complain to his guide: 'You've brought us all the way to the top of this forsaken mountain, and what have you shown us? The kabristan!'

True, the old British graves are all that one can see through the fog. Some of the tombstones have been standing there for close to two centuries. The old abandoned parsonage next door to the cemetery is now the home of Victor Banerjee, the celebrated actor. He enjoys living next door to the graveyard, and one night he defied me to walk home alone past the graves. I am not a superstitious person but I did feel rather uneasy as those old graves loomed up through the mist. I was startled by the cry of a night-bird emanating from behind one of the tombstones. Then a weird, blood-chilling cry rose from a clump of bushes. It was Victor, trying to frighten me—or possibly practising for his next role as Dracula. I was about to break into a run when a large dog—one of our strays—appeared beside me and accompanied me home. On a dark and scary night, even a half-starved mongrel is welcome company. By day, the road holds no terrors. But there are other hazards. On the road near Char Dukan, several small boys are kicking a football around. The ball rolls temptingly towards me. Remembering my football skills of fifty or more years ago, I cannot resist the temptation to put boot to ball. I give it a mighty kick. The ball sails away, the children applaud, I am left hopping about on the road in agony, I had quite forgotten my gout! I'm glad I stuck to writing instead of taking up professional football. At seventy I can still write without inflicting damage on myself.

∽

When I am feeling good, and have the road to myself, I do occasionally break into song. This is the only opportunity I have to sing. Otherwise my musical abilities turn friends into foes.

I am not permitted to sing in the homes of my friends. If I am being driven about in their cars, I am told to remain silent unless we veer off the road or hit an oncoming vehicle. Even at home, the sound of my music causes the girls to drop dishes and the children to find an excuse to stop doing their homework.

'Dada is ill again,' says Gautam, when all I am trying to do is emulate Caruso singing 'Che Gelida Nlanina' (Your Tiny Hand is Frozen) from *La Bohème*. Our tiny hands do freeze up here in the winter, and there's nothing like an operatic aria to get the blood circulating freely. Of course Caruso was a tenor, but I can also sing baritone like Domingo or Nelson Eddy and bass like Chaliapin the great Russian singer. Sometimes I combine all three voices—tenor, baritone, and bass—that's when the window glass shatters and cars come to a screeching halt.

It was a boyhood ambition to be an opera star, but I'm afraid I never made it beyond the school choir. Our music teacher did not appreciate the wide range of my voice. 'Too loud!' she would screech. 'Too flat!'

'Caruso sings in A-flat,' I replied.

'You sound like a warbling frog,' she snapped. 'And

you look like one,' I responded.

And that was the end of my brief appearance in cassock and surplice.

But when I'm on the open road—especially when it's raining and I have the road to myself—I am free to sing as loud and as flat as I like, and if flat tyres on passing cars are the result, it's the fault of the tyres and not my singing.

So here we go:

When you are down and out,
Lift up your head and shout—
It's going to be a great day!

There's nothing like a spirited song to raise the flagging spirit. Whenever I feel down and out—and that's often enough—I recall some old favourite and share it with the trees, the birds, and even those pesky monkeys.

Just like a sunflower
After a summer shower
My inspiration is you!

Sloppy, sentimental stuff, but it works.

And there's always the likelihood of a little romance around the corner.

Some enchanted evening
You will see a stranger
Across a crowded room....

Actually, I prefer the winding road to a crowded room. Romantic encounters are more likely when there are not too many people around. Such as the other day, when I had unfurled my new umbrella and was sauntering up the road, singing my favourite rain song, 'Singing in the Rain'.

I had gone some distance when I noticed a young lady struggling up the road a little way ahead of me. My glasses were wet and misty, but I was determined to share my umbrella with any damsel in distress. So, huffing and puffing, I caught up with her.

'Do share my umbrella,' I offered.

No, she wasn't sweet twenty-one, as I'd hoped. She was nearer eighty. But she was munching on a bhutta, so her teeth were in good order. She took the umbrella from me and munched on ahead, leaving me to get drenched. A retired headmistress, as I discovered later!

She returned the umbrella when we got to Char Dukan, but in future I shall make a frontal approach before making any gallant overtures on the road. Those crowded rooms are safer.

Monsoon time, and umbrellas are taken out and frequently lost. I lost three last year. One was borrowed, and as you know, borrowed books and umbrellas are seldom returned. By some mysterious process they become the permanent property of the borrower. Another disappeared while I was cashing a cheque in the bank. And the third was wrecked in the following fashion.

Coming down from Char Dukan, I found two hefty boys engaged in furious combat in the middle of the road. One was a kick-boxer, the other a kung fu exponent. Afraid that one of them would be badly hurt, I decided to intervene, and called out, 'Come on boys, break it up!' I thrust my umbrella between them in a bid to end the fracas. My umbrella received a mighty kick, and went sailing across the road and over the parapet. The boys stopped fighting in order to laugh at my discomfiture. One of them retrieved my umbrella, minus its handle.

In a way, I'd been successful as a peacemaker—certainly more successful than the United Nations—although at some cost to my personal property. Well, we peacemakers must be prepared to put up with a little inconvenience.

I'm a great believer in the Law of Compensation (as propounded by Emerson in his famous essay)—that what we do, good or bad, is returned in full measure in this life rather than in the hereafter.

Not long after the incident just described, there was my old friend Vipin Buckshey standing on the threshold with a seasonal gift—a beautiful blue umbrella!

He did not know about the street-fight but had read my story 'The Blue Umbrella'—a simple tale about greed being overcome by generosity—and had bought me a blue umbrella in appreciation. I shall be careful not to lose it.

THE LEOPARD

I first saw the leopard when I was crossing the small stream at the bottom of the hill.

The ravine was so deep that for most of the day it remained in shadow. This encouraged many birds and animals to emerge from cover during the daylight hours. Few people ever passed that way: only milkmen and charcoal burners from the surrounding villages. As a result, the ravine had become a little haven for wildlife, one of the few natural sanctuaries left near Mussoorie.

Below my cottage was a forest of oak and maple and Himalayan rhododendron. A narrow path twisted its way down through the trees, over an open ridge where red sorrel grew wild, and then steeply down through a tangle of wild raspberries, creeping vines, and slender bamboo. At the bottom of the hill the path led on to a grassy verge, surrounded by wild dog roses. (It is surprising how closely the flora of the lower Himalayas, between 5,000 and 8,000 feet, resembles that of the English countryside.)

The stream ran close by the verge, tumbling over smooth pebbles, over rocks worn yellow with age, on its way to the plains and to the little Song River and finally to the sacred Ganga River.

When I first discovered the stream, it was early April

and the wild roses were flowering—small white blossoms lying in clusters.

I walked down to the stream almost every day after two or three hours of writing. I had lived in cities too long and had returned to the hills to renew myself, both physically and mentally. Once you have lived with mountains for any length of time you belong to them, and must return again and again.

Nearly every morning, and sometimes during the day, I heard the cry of the barking deer. And in the evening, walking through the forest, I disturbed parties of pheasants. The birds went gliding down the ravine on open, motionless wings. I saw pine martens and a handsome red fox, and I recognized the footprints of a bear.

As I had not come to take anything from the forest, the birds and animals soon grew accustomed to my presence; or possibly they recognized my footsteps. After some time, my approach did not disturb them.

The langurs in the oak and rhododendron trees, who would at first go leaping through the branches at my approach, now watched me with some curiosity as they munched the tender green shoots of the oak. The young ones scuffled and wrestled like boys while their parents groomed each other's coats, stretching themselves out on the sunlit hillside.

But one evening, as I passed, I heard them chattering in the trees, and I knew I was not the cause of their excitement. As I crossed the stream and began climbing the hill, the grunting and chattering increased, as though the langurs were trying to warn me of some hidden danger. A shower of pebbles came rattling down the steep hillside, and I looked up to see a sinewy, orange-gold leopard poised on a rock about twenty feet above me.

He was not looking towards me but had his head thrust attentively forward, in the direction of the ravine. Yet he must have sensed my presence, because, he slowly turned his head and looked down at me.

He seemed a little puzzled at my presence there; and when, to give myself courage, I clapped my hands sharply, the leopard sprang away into the thickets, making absolutely no sound as he melted into the shadows.

I had disturbed the animal in his quest for food. But a little after I heard the quickening cry of a barking deer as it fled through the forest. The hunt was still on.

The leopard, like other members of the cat family, is nearing extinction in India, and I was surprised to find one so close to Mussoorie. Probably the deforestation that had been taking place in the surrounding hills had driven the deer into this green valley; and the leopard, naturally, had followed.

It was some weeks before I saw the leopard again, although I was often made aware of its presence. A dry, rasping cough sometimes gave it away. At times I felt almost certain that I was being followed.

Once, when I was late getting home, and the brief twilight gave way to a dark moonless night, I was startled by a family of porcupines running about in a clearing. I looked around nervously and saw two bright eyes staring at me from a thicket. I stood still, my heart banging away against my ribs. Then the eyes danced away and I realized that they were only fireflies.

In May and June, when the hills are brown and dry, it is always cool and green near the stream, where ferns and maidenhair and long grasses continue to thrive.

Downstream I found a small pool where I could bathe, and a cave with water dripping from the roof, the water spangled gold and silver in the shafts of sunlight that pushed through the slits in the cave roof.

'He maketh me to lie down in green pastures; he leadeth me beside the still waters.' Perhaps David had discovered a similar paradise when he wrote those words; perhaps I, too, would write good words. The hill station's summer visitors had not discovered this haven of wild and green things. I was beginning to feel that the place belonged to me, that dominion was mine.

The stream had at least one other regular visitor, a spotted forktail, and though it did not fly away at my approach, it became restless if I stayed too long, and then she would move from boulder to boulder uttering a long complaining cry.

I spent an afternoon trying to discover the bird's nest, which I was certain contained young ones, because I had seen the forktail carrying grubs in her bill. The problem was that when the bird flew upstream, I had difficulty in following her rapidly enough as the rocks were sharp and slippery.

Eventually I decorated myself with bracken fronds and, after slowly making my way upstream, hid myself in the hollow stump of a tree at a spot where the forktail often disappeared. I had no intention of robbing the bird. I was simply curious to see its home.

By crouching down, I was able to command a view of a small stretch of the stream and the side of the ravine; but I had done little to deceive the forktail, who continued to object strongly to my presence so near her home.

I summoned up my reserves of patience and sat perfectly still for about ten minutes. The forktail quietened down. Out of sight, out of mind. But where had she gone? Probably into the walls of the ravine where, I felt sure, she was guarding her nest.

I decided to take her by surprise and stood up suddenly, in time to see not the forktail on her doorstep but the leopard bounding away with a grunt of surprise! Two urgent springs, and he had crossed the stream and plunged into the forest.

I was as astonished as the leopard, and forgot all about the forktail and her nest. Had the leopard been following me again?

I decided against this possibility. Only man-eaters follow humans and, as far as I knew, there had never been a man-eater in the vicinity of Mussoorie.

During the monsoon the stream became a rushing torrent; bushes and small trees were swept away, and the friendly murmur of the water became a threatening boom. I did not visit the place too often as there were leeches in the long grass.

One day I found the remains of a barking deer, which had only been partly eaten. I wondered why the leopard had not hidden the rest of his meal, and decided that it must have been disturbed while eating.

Then, climbing the hill, I met a party of hunters resting beneath the oaks. They asked me if I had seen a leopard. I said I had not. They said they knew there was a leopard in the forest.

Leopard skins, they told me, were selling in Delhi at over a thousand rupees each. Of course there was a ban on the export of skins, but they gave me to understand that there were ways and means.... I thanked them for their information and walked on, feeling uneasy and disturbed.

The hunters had seen the carcass of the deer, and they had seen the leopard's pug marks, and they kept coming to the forest. Almost every evening I heard their guns banging away; for they were ready to fire at almost anything.

'There's a leopard about,' they always told me.

'You should carry a gun.'

'I don't have one,' I said.

There were fewer birds to be seen, and even the langurs had moved on. The red fox did not show itself; and the pine martens, who had become quite bold, now dashed into hiding at my approach. The smell of one human is like the smell of any other.

And then the rains were over and it was October. I could lie in the sun, on sweet-smelling grass, and gaze up through a pattern of oak leaves into a blinding blue heaven. And I would praise God for leaves and grass and the smell of things—the smell of mint and bruised clover—and the touch of things—the touch of grass and air and sky, the touch of the sky's blueness.

I thought no more of the men. My attitude towards them was similar to that of the denizens of the forest. These were men, unpredictable, and to be avoided if possible.

On the other side of the ravine rose Pari Tibba, Hill of the Fairies; a bleak, scrub-covered hill where no one lived.

It was said that in the previous century Englishmen had tried building their houses on the hill, but the area had always attracted lightning, due to either the hill's location or due to its mineral deposits; after several houses had been struck by lighting, the settlers had moved on to the next hill, where the town now stands.

To the hillmen it is Pari Tibba, haunted by the spirits of a pair of ill-fated lovers who perished there in a storm; to others it is known as Burnt Hill, because of its scarred and stunted trees.

One day, after crossing the stream, I climbed Pari Tibba—a stiff undertaking, because there was no path to the top and I had to scramble up a precipitous rock face with the help of rocks and roots that were apt to come loose in my groping hand.

But at the top was a plateau with a few pine trees, their upper branches catching the wind and humming softly. There I found the ruins of what must have been the houses of the first settlers—just a few piles of rubble, now overgrown with weeds, sorrel, dandelions, and nettles.

As I walked though the roofless ruins, I was struck by the silence that surrounded me, the absence of birds and animals, the sense of complete desolation.

The silence was so absolute that it seemed to be ringing in my ears. But there was something else of which I was becoming increasingly aware: the strong feline odour of one of the cat family. I paused and looked about. I was alone. There was no movement of dry leaf or loose stone.

The ruins were for the most part open to the sky. Their rotting rafters had collapsed, jamming together to form a low passage like the entrance to a mine; and this dark cavern seemed to lead down into the ground. The smell was stronger when I approached this spot, so I stopped again and waited there, wondering if I had discovered the lair of the leopard, wondering if the animal was now at rest after a night's hunt.

Perhaps he was crouching there in the dark, watching me, recognizing me, knowing me as the man who walked alone in the forest without a weapon.

I like to think that he was there, that he knew me, and that he acknowledged my visit in the friendliest way: by ignoring me altogether.

Perhaps I had made him confident—too confident, too careless, too trusting of the human in his midst. I did not venture any further; I was not out of my mind. I did not seek physical contact, or even another glimpse of that beautiful sinewy body, springing from rock to rock. It was his trust I wanted, and I think he gave it to me.

But did the leopard, trusting one man, make the mistake of bestowing his trust on others? Did I, by casting out all fear—my own fear, and the leopard's protective fear—leave him defenceless? Because the next day, coming up the path from the stream, shouting and beating drums, were the hunters. They had a long bamboo pole across their shoulders; and slung from the pole, feet up, head down, was the lifeless body of the leopard, shot in the neck and in the head.

'We told you there was a leopard!' they shouted, in great good humour. 'Isn't he a fine specimen?'

'Yes,' I said. 'He was a beautiful leopard.'

I walked home through the silent forest. It was very silent, almost as though the birds and animals knew that their trust had been violated.

I remembered the lines of a poem by D. H. Lawrence; and, as I climbed the steep and lonely path to my home, the words beat out their rhythm in my mind: 'There was room in the world for a mountain lion and me.'

PANTHER'S MOON

I

In the entire village, he was the first to get up. Even the dog, a big hill mastiff called Sheroo, was asleep in a corner of the dark room, curled up near the cold embers of the previous night's fire. Bisnu's tousled head emerged from his blanket. He rubbed the sleep from his eyes and sat up on his haunches. Then, gathering his wits, he crawled in the direction of the loud ticking that came from the battered little clock which occupied the second most honoured place in a niche in the wall. The most honoured place belonged to a picture of Ganesha, the god of learning, who had an elephant's head and a fat boy's body. Bringing his face close to the clock, Bisnu could just make out the hands. It was five o'clock. He had half an hour in which to get ready and leave.

He got up, in vest and underpants, and moved quietly towards the door. The soft tread of his bare feet woke Sheroo and the big black dog rose silently and padded behind the boy. The door opened and closed and then the boy and the dog were outside in the early dawn. The month was June and the nights were warm, even in the Himalayan valleys, but there was fresh dew on

169

the grass. Bisnu felt the dew beneath his feet. He took a deep breath and began walking down to the stream.

The sound of the stream filled the small valley. At that early hour of the morning, it was the only sound; but Bisnu was hardly conscious of it. It was a sound he lived with and took for granted. It was only when he had crossed the hill, on his way to the town—and the sound of the stream grew distant—that he really began to notice it. And it was only when the stream was too far away to be heard that he really missed its sound.

He slipped out of his underclothes, gazed for a few moments at the goose pimples rising on his flesh, and then dashed into the shallow stream. As he went further in, the cold mountain water reached his loins and navel and he gasped with shock and pleasure. He drifted slowly with the current, swam across to a small inlet which formed a fairly deep pool and plunged into the water. Sheroo hated cold water at this early hour. Had the sun been up, he would not have hesitated to join Bisnu. Now he contented himself with sitting on a smooth rock and gazing placidly at the slim brown boy splashing about in the clear water, in the widening light of dawn.

Bisnu did not stay long in the water. There wasn't time. When he returned to the house, he found his mother up, making tea and chapattis. His sister, Puja, was still asleep. She was a little older than Bisnu, a pretty girl with large black eyes, good teeth, and strong arms and legs. During the day, she helped her mother in the house and in the fields. She did not go to the school with Bisnu. But when he came home in the evenings, he would try teaching her some of the things he had learnt. Their father was dead. Bisnu, at twelve, considered himself the head of the family.

He ate two chapattis, after spreading butter-oil on them. He drank a glass of hot, sweet tea. His mother gave two thick chapattis to Sheroo and the dog wolfed them down in a few minutes. Then she wrapped two chapattis and a gourd curry in some big green leaves and handed these to Bisnu. This was his lunch packet. His mother and Puja would take their meal afterwards.

When Bisnu was dressed, he stood with folded hands before the picture of Ganesha. Ganesha is the god who blesses all beginnings. The author who begins to write a new book, the banker who opens a new ledger, the traveller who starts on a journey, all invoke the kindly help of Ganesha. And as Bisnu made a journey every day, he never left without the goodwill of the elephant-headed god.

How, one might ask, did Ganesha get his elephant's head? When born, he was a beautiful child. Parvati, his mother, was so proud of him that she went about showing him to everyone.

Unfortunately, she made the mistake of showing the child to that envious planet, Saturn, who promptly burnt off poor Ganesha's head. Parvati in despair went to Brahma, the Creator, for a new head for her son. He had no head to give her but advised her to search for some man or animal caught in a sinful or wrong act. Parvati wandered about until she came upon an elephant sleeping with its head the wrong way, that is, to the south. She promptly removed the elephant's head and planted it on Ganesha's shoulders, where it took root.

Bisnu knew this story. He had heard it from his mother. Wearing a white shirt and black shorts and a pair of worn white keds, he was ready for his long walk to school, five miles up the mountain.

His sister woke up just as he was about to leave. She pushed the hair away from her face and gave Bisnu one of her rare smiles.

'I hope you have not forgotten,' she said.

'Forgotten?' said Bisnu, pretending innocence. 'Is there anything I am supposed to remember?'

'Don't tease me. You promised to buy me a pair of bangles, remember? I hope you won't spend the money on sweets, as you did last time.'

'Oh, yes, your bangles,' said Bisnu. 'Girls have nothing better to do than waste money on trinkets. Now, don't lose your temper! I'll get them for you. Red and gold are the colours you want?'

'Yes, Brother,' said Puja gently, pleased that Bisnu had remembered the colours.

'And for your dinner tonight we'll make you something special. Won't we, Mother?'

'Yes. But hurry up and dress. There is some ploughing to be done today. The rains will soon be here, if the gods are kind.'

'The monsoon will be late this year,' said Bisnu. 'Mr Nautiyal, our teacher, told us so. He said it had nothing to do with the gods.'

'Be off, you are getting late,' said Puja, before Bisnu

could begin an argument with his mother. She was diligently winding the old clock. It was quite light in the room. The sun would be up any minute.

Bisnu shouldered his school bag, kissed his mother, pinched his sister's cheeks, and left the house. He started climbing the steep path up the mountainside. Sheroo bounded ahead; for he, too, always went with Bisnu to school.

Five miles to school. Every day, except Sunday, Bisnu walked five miles to school; and in the evening, he walked home again. There was no school in his own small village of Manjari, for the village consisted of only five families. The nearest school was at Kempty, a small township on the bus route through the district of Garhwal. A number of boys walked to school, from distances of two or three miles; their villages were not quite as remote as Manjari. But Bisnu's village lay right at the bottom of the mountain, a drop of over two thousand feet from Kempty. There was no proper road between the village and the town.

In Kempty there was a school, a small mission hospital, a post office, and several shops. In Manjari village there were none of these amenities. If you were sick, you stayed at home until you got well; if you were very sick, you walked or were carried to the hospital, up the five-mile path. If you wanted to buy something, you went without it; but if you wanted it very badly, you could walk the five miles to Kempty.

Manjari was known as the Five-Mile Village.

Twice a week, if there were any letters, a postman

came to the village. Bisnu usually passed the postman on his way to and from school.

There were other boys in Manjari village, but Bisnu was the only one who went to school. His mother would not have fussed if he had stayed at home and worked in the fields. That was what the other boys did; all except lazy Chittru, who preferred fishing in the stream or helping himself to the fruit off other people's trees. But Bisnu went to school. He went because he wanted to. No one could force him to go; and no one could stop him from going. He had set his heart on receiving a good schooling. He wanted to read and write as well as anyone in the big world, the world that seemed to begin only where the mountains ended. He felt cut off from the world in his small valley. He would rather live at the top of a mountain than at the bottom of one. That was why he liked climbing to Kempty, it took him to the top of the mountain; and from its ridge he could look down on his own valley to the north and to the wide, endless plains stretching towards the south.

The plainsman looks to the hills for the needs of his spirit but the hillman looks to the plains for a living. Leaving the village and the fields below him, Bisnu climbed steadily up the bare hillside, now dry and brown. By the time the sun was up, he had entered the welcome shade of an oak and rhododendron forest. Sheroo went bounding ahead, chasing squirrels and barking at langurs.

A colony of langurs lived in the oak forest. They fed on oak leaves, acorns, and other green things, and usually remained in the trees, coming down to the ground only to play or bask in the sun. They were beautiful, supple-limbed animals, with black faces and silver-grey coats and long, sensitive tails. They leapt from tree to tree with great agility. The young ones wrestled on the grass like boys.

A dignified community, the langurs did not have the cheekiness or dishonest habits of the red monkeys of the plains; they did not approach dogs or humans. But they had grown used to Bisnu's comings and goings and did not fear him. Some of the older ones would watch him quietly, a little puzzled. They did not go near the town, because the Kempty boys threw stones at them. And anyway, the oak forest gave them all the food they required. Emerging from the trees, Bisnu crossed a small brook. Here he stopped to drink the fresh clean water of a spring. The brook tumbled down the mountain and joined the river a little below Bisnu's village. Coming from another direction was a second path and at the junction of the two paths Sarru was waiting for him. Sarru came from a small village about three miles from Bisnu's and closer to the town. He had two large milk cans slung over his shoulders. Every morning he carried this milk to town, selling one can to the school and the other to Mrs Taylor, the lady doctor at the small mission hospital. He was a little older than Bisnu but not as well built.

They hailed each other and Sarru fell into step beside Bisnu. They often met at this spot, keeping each other company for the remaining two miles to Kempty.

'There was a panther in our village last night,' said Sarru.

This information interested but did not excite Bisnu. Panthers were common enough in the hills and did not usually present a problem except during the winter months, when their natural prey was scarce. Then, occasionally, a panther would take to haunting the outskirts of a village, seizing a careless dog or a stray goat.

'Did you lose any animals?' asked Bisnu.

'No. It tried to get into the cowshed but the dogs set off an alarm. We drove it off.'

'It must be the same one which came around last winter. We lost a calf and two dogs in our village.'

'Wasn't that the one the shikaris wounded? I hope it hasn't become a cattle lifter.'

'It could be the same. It has a bullet in its leg. These hunters are the people who cause all the trouble. They think it's easy to shoot a panther. It would be better if they missed altogether but they usually wound it.'

'And then the panther's too slow to catch the barking deer and starts on our own animals.'

'We're lucky it didn't become a man-eater. Do you remember the man-eater six years ago? I was very small then. My father told me all about it. Ten people were killed in our valley alone. What happened to it?'

'I don't know. Some say it poisoned itself when it ate the headman of another village.'

Bisnu laughed. 'No one liked that old villain. He must have been a man-eater himself in some previous existence!' They linked arms and scrambled up the stony path. Sheroo began barking and ran ahead. Someone was coming down the path. It was Mela Ram, the postman.

II

'Any letters for us?' asked Bisnu and Sarru together. They never received any letters but that did not stop them from asking. It was one way of finding out who had received letters.

'You're welcome to all of them,' said Mela Ram, 'if you'll carry my bag for me.'

'Not today,' said Sarru. 'We're busy today. Is there a letter from Corporal Ghanshyam for his family?'

'Yes, there is a postcard for his people. He is posted on the Ladakh border now and finds it very cold there.'

Postcards, unlike sealed letters, were considered public property and were read by everyone. The senders knew that too, and so Corporal Ghanshyam Singh was careful to mention that he expected a promotion very soon. He wanted everyone in his village to know it.

Mela Ram, complaining of sore feet, continued on his way and the boys carried on up the path. It was eight o'clock when they reached Kempty. Dr Taylor's outpatients were just beginning to trickle in at the hospital gate. The doctor was trying to prop up a rose creeper which had blown down during the night. She liked attending to her plants in the mornings, before starting on her patients. She found this helped her in her work. There was a lot in common between ailing plants and ailing people.

Dr Taylor was fifty, white-haired but fresh in the face, and full of vitality. She had been in India for twenty years and ten of these had been spent working in the hill regions.

She saw Bisnu coming down the road. She knew

about the boy and his long walk to school and admired him for his keenness and sense of purpose. She wished there were more like him.

Bisnu greeted her shyly. Sheroo barked and put his paws up on the gate.

'Yes, there's a bone for you,' said Dr Taylor. She often put aside bones for the big black dog, for she knew that Bisnu's people could not afford to give the dog a regular diet of meat—though he did well enough on milk and chapattis.

She threw the bone over the gate and Sheroo caught it before it fell. The school bell began ringing and Bisnu broke into a run.

Sheroo loped along behind the boy.

When Bisnu entered the school gate, Sheroo sat down on the grass of the compound. He would remain there until the lunch break. He knew of various ways of amusing himself during school hours and had friends among the bazaar dogs. But just then he didn't want company. He had his bone to get on with.

Mr Nautiyal, Bisnu's teacher, was in a bad mood. He was a keen rose grower and only that morning, on getting up and looking out of his bedroom window, he had been horrified to see a herd of goats in his garden. He had chased them down the road with a stick but the damage had already been done. His prize roses had all been consumed.

Mr Nautiyal had been so upset that he had gone without his breakfast. He had also cut himself whilst shaving. Thus, his mood had gone from bad to worse.

Several times during the day, he brought down his ruler on the knuckles of any boy who irritated him. Bisnu was one of his best pupils. But even Bisnu irritated him by asking too many questions about a new sum which Mr Nautiyal didn't feel like explaining.

That was the kind of day it was for Mr Nautiyal. Most schoolteachers know similar days.

'Poor Mr Nautiyal,' thought Bisnu. 'I wonder why he's so upset. It must be because of his pay. He doesn't get much money. But he's a good teacher. I hope he doesn't take another job.'

But after Mr Nautiyal had eaten his lunch, his mood improved (as it always did after a meal) and the rest of the day passed serenely. Armed with a bundle of homework, Bisnu came out from the school compound at four o'clock and was immediately joined by Sheroo. He proceeded down the road in the company of several of his class-fellows. But he did not linger long in the bazaar. There were five miles to walk and he did not like to get home too late. Usually, he reached his house just as it was beginning to get dark.

Sarru had gone home long ago and Bisnu had to make the return journey on his own. It was a good opportunity to memorize the words of an English poem he had been asked to learn. Bisnu had reached the little brook when he remembered the bangles he had promised to buy for his sister.

'Oh, I've forgotten them again,' he said aloud. 'Now I'll catch it—and she's probably made something special for my dinner!'

Sheroo, to whom these words were addressed, paid no attention but bounded off into the oak forest. Bisnu looked around for the monkeys but they were nowhere to be seen.

'Strange,' he thought, 'I wonder why they have disappeared.'

He was startled by a sudden sharp cry, followed by a fierce yelp. He knew at once that Sheroo was in trouble. The noise came from the bushes down the khud, into which the dog had rushed but a few seconds previously.

Bisnu jumped off the path and ran down the slope towards the bushes. There was no dog and not a sound. He whistled and called but there was no response. Then he saw something lying on the dry grass. He picked it up. It was a portion of a dog's collar, stained with blood. It was Sheroo's collar and Sheroo's blood.

Bisnu did not search further. He knew, without a doubt, that Sheroo had been seized by a panther. No other animal could have attacked so silently and swiftly and carried off a big dog without a struggle. Sheroo was dead—must have been dead within seconds of being caught and flung into the air. Bisnu knew the danger that lay in wait for him if he followed the blood trail through the trees. The panther would attack anyone who interfered with its meal.

With tears starting in his eyes, Bisnu carried on down the path to the village. His fingers still clutched the little bit of bloodstained collar that was all that was left to him of his dog.

III

Bisnu was not a very sentimental boy but he sorrowed for his dog who had been his companion on many a hike into the hills and forests. He did not sleep that night but turned restlessly from side to side, moaning softly. After some time he felt Puja's hand on his head. She began stroking his brow. He took her hand in his own and the clasp of her rough, warm, familiar hand gave him a feeling of comfort and security.

Next morning, when he went down to the stream to bathe, he missed the presence of his dog. He did not stay long in the water. It wasn't as much fun when there was no Sheroo to watch him.

When Bisnu's mother gave him his food, she told him to be careful and hurry home that evening. A panther, even if it is only a cowardly lifter of sheep or dogs, is not to be trifled with. And this particular panther had shown some daring by seizing the dog even before it was dark.

Still, there was no question of staying away from school. If Bisnu remained at home every time a panther put in an appearance, he might just as well stop going to school altogether.

He set off even earlier than usual and reached the meeting of the paths long before Sarru. He did not wait for his friend because he did not feel like talking about the loss of his dog. It was not the day for the postman and so Bisnu reached Kempty without meeting anyone on the way. He tried creeping past the hospital gate unnoticed, but Dr Taylor saw him and the first thing she said was: 'Where's Sheroo? I've got something for him.'

When Dr Taylor saw the boy's face, she knew at once that something was wrong.

'What is it, Bisnu?' she asked. She looked quickly up and down the road. 'Is it Sheroo?'

He nodded gravely.

'A panther took him,' he said.

'In the village?'

'No, while we were walking home through the forest. I did not see anything—but I heard.'

Dr Taylor knew that there was nothing she could say that would console him and she tried to conceal the bone which she had brought out for the dog, but Bisnu noticed her hiding it behind her back and the tears welled up in his eyes. He turned away and began running down the road.

His schoolfellows noticed Sheroo's absence and questioned Bisnu. He had to tell them everything. They were full of sympathy but they were also quite thrilled at what had happened and kept pestering Bisnu for all the details. There was a lot of noise in the classroom, and Mr Nautiyal had to call for order. When he learnt what had happened, he patted Bisnu on the head and told him that he need not attend school for the rest of the day. But Bisnu did not want to go home. After school, he got into a fight with one of the boys, and that helped him forget.

IV

The panther that plunged the village into an atmosphere of gloom and terror may not have been the same panther that took Sheroo. There was no way of knowing and it would have made no difference, because the panther that came by night and struck at the people of Manjari was that most feared of wild creatures, a man-eater.

Nine-year-old Sanjay, son of Kalam Singh, was the first child to be attacked by the panther.

Kalam Singh's house was the last in the village and nearest the stream. Like the other houses, it was quite small, just a room above and a stable below, with steps leading up from outside the house. He lived there with his wife, two sons (Sanjay was the youngest), and little daughter Basanti, who had just turned three.

Sanjay had brought his father's cows home after grazing them on the hillside in the company of other children. He had also brought home an edible wild plant, which his mother cooked into a tasty dish for their evening meal. They had their food at dusk, sitting on the floor of their single room, and soon after settled down for the night. Sanjay curled up in his favourite spot, with his head near the door, where he got a little fresh air. As the nights were warm, the door was usually left a little ajar. Sanjay's mother piled ash on the embers of the fire and the family was soon asleep.

No one heard the stealthy padding of a panther approaching the door, pushing it wider open. But suddenly there were sounds of a frantic struggle, and Sanjay's stifled cries were mixed with the grunts of the panther. Kalam Singh leapt to his feet with a shout. The panther had dragged Sanjay out of the door and was pulling him down the steps, when Kalam Singh started battering at the animal with a large stone. The rest of the family screamed in terror, rousing the entire village. A number of men came to Kalam Singh's assistance and the panther was driven off. But Sanjay lay unconscious.

Someone brought a lantern and the boy's mother screamed when she saw her small son with his head lying in a pool of blood. It looked as if the side of his head had been eaten off by the panther. But he was still alive, and as Kalam Singh plastered ash on the boy's head to stop the bleeding, he found that though the scalp had been torn off one side of the head, the bare bone was smooth and unbroken.

'He won't live through the night,' said a neighbour. 'We'll have to carry him down to the river in the morning.'

The dead were always cremated on the banks of a small river which flowed past Manjari village.

Suddenly, the panther, still prowling about the village, called out in rage and frustration, and the villagers rushed to their homes in panic and barricaded themselves in for the night.

Sanjay's mother sat by the boy for the rest of the night, weeping and watching. Towards dawn he started to moan and show signs of coming round. At this sign of returning consciousness, Kalam Singh rose determinedly and looked around for his stick.

He told his elder son to remain behind with the mother and daughter, as he was going to take Sanjay to Dr Taylor at the hospital.

'See, he is moaning and in pain,' said Kalam Singh.

'That means he has a chance to live if he can be treated at once.'

With a stout stick in his hand, and Sanjay on his back, Kalam Singh set off on the two miles of hard mountain track to the hospital at Kempty. His son, a bloodstained cloth around his head, was moaning but still unconscious. When at last Kalam Singh climbed up through the last fields below the hospital, he asked for the doctor and stammered out an account of what had happened.

It was a terrible injury, as Dr Taylor discovered. The bone over almost one-third of the head was bare and the scalp was torn all around. As the father told his story, the doctor cleaned and dressed the wound, and then gave Sanjay a shot of penicillin to prevent sepsis. Later, Kalam Singh carried the boy home again.

V

After this, the panther went away for some time. But the people of Manjari could not be sure of its whereabouts. They kept to their houses after dark and shut their doors. Bisnu had to stop going to school, because there was no one to accompany him and it was dangerous to go alone. This worried him because his final exam was only a few weeks away and he would be missing important classwork. When he wasn't in the fields, helping with the sowing of rice and maize, he would be sitting in the shade of a chestnut tree, going through his well-thumbed second-hand schoolbooks. He had no other reading, except for a copy of the Ramayana and a Hindi translation of *Alice in Wonderland*. These were well preserved, read only in fits and starts and usually kept locked in his mother's old tin trunk.

Sanjay had nightmares for several nights and woke up screaming. But with the resilience of youth, he quickly recovered. At the end of the week he was able to walk to the hospital, though his father always accompanied him. Even a desperate panther will hesitate to attack a party of two. Sanjay, with his thin, little face and huge bandaged head, looked a pathetic figure, but he was getting better and the wound looked like it was healing.

Bisnu often went to see him, and the two boys spent long hours together near the stream. Sometimes Chittru would join them, and they would try catching fish with a homemade net. They were often successful in taking home one or two mountain trout. Sometimes, Bisnu and Chittru wrestled in the shallow water or on the grassy banks of the stream. Chittru was a chubby boy with a broad chest, strong legs and thighs, and when he used his weight he got Bisnu under him. But Bisnu was hard and wiry and had very strong wrists and fingers. When he had Chittru in a vice, the bigger boy would cry out and give up the struggle. Sanjay could not join in these games.

He had never been a very strong boy and he needed plenty of rest if his wounds were to heal well.

The panther had not been seen for over a week and the people of Manjari were beginning to hope that it might have moved on over the mountain or further down the valley.

'I think I can start going to school again,' said Bisnu.

'The panther has gone away.'

'Don't be too sure,' said Puja. 'The moon is full these days and perhaps it is only being cautious.'

'Wait a few days,' said their mother. 'It is better to wait. Perhaps you could go the day after tomorrow when Sanjay goes to the hospital with his father. Then you will not be alone.'

And so, two days later, Bisnu went up to Kempty with Sanjay and Kalam Singh. Sanjay's wound had almost healed over. Little islets of flesh had grown over the bone. Dr Taylor told him that he need come to see her only once a fortnight, instead of every third day.

Bisnu went to his school and was given a warm welcome by his friends and by Mr Nautiyal.

'You'll have to work hard,' said his teacher. 'You have to catch up with the others. If you like, I can give you some extra time after classes.'

'Thank you, sir, but it will make me late,' said Bisnu. 'I must get home before it is dark, otherwise my mother will worry. I think the panther has gone but nothing is certain.'

'Well, you mustn't take risks. Do your best, Bisnu. Work hard and you'll soon catch up with your lessons.'

Sanjay and Kalam Singh were waiting for him outside the school. Together they took the path down to Manjari, passing the postman on the way. Mela Ram said he had heard that the panther was in another district and that there was nothing to fear. He was on his rounds again.

Nothing happened on the way. The langurs were back in their favourite part of the forest. Bisnu got home just as the kerosene lamp was being lit. Puja met him at the door with a winsome smile.

'Did you get the bangles?' she asked.

But Bisnu had forgotten again.

VI

There had been a thunderstorm and some rain—a short, sharp shower which gave the villagers hope that the monsoon would arrive on time. It brought out the thunder lilies—pink, crocus-like flowers which sprang up on the hillsides immediately after a summer shower.

Bisnu, on his way home from school, was caught in the rain. He knew the shower would not last, so he took shelter in a small cave and, to pass the time, began doing sums, scratching figures in the damp earth with the end of a stick.

When the rain stopped, he came out from the cave and continued down the path. He wasn't in a hurry. The rain had made everything smell fresh and good. The scent from fallen pine needles rose from the wet earth. The leaves of the oak trees had been washed clean and a light breeze turned them about, showing their silver undersides. The birds, refreshed and high-spirited, set up a terrific noise. The worst offenders were the yellow-bottomed bulbuls who squabbled and fought in the blackberry bushes. A barbet, high up in the branches of a deodar, set up its querulous, plaintive call. And a flock of bright green parrots came swooping down the hill to settle on a wild plum tree and feast on the unripe fruit. The langurs, too, had been revived by the rain. They leapt friskily from tree to tree, greeting Bisnu with little grunts.

He was almost out of the oak forest when he heard a faint bleating. Presently, a little goat came stumbling up the path towards him. The kid was far from home and must have strayed from the rest of the herd. But it was not yet conscious of being lost. It came to Bisnu with a hop, skip, and jump and started nuzzling against his legs like a cat.

'I wonder who you belong to,' mused Bisnu, stroking the little creature. 'You'd better come home with me until someone claims you.'

He didn't have to take the kid in his arms. It was used to humans and followed close at his heels. Now that darkness was coming on, Bisnu walked a little faster.

He had not gone very far when he heard the sawing grunt of a panther.

The sound came from the hill to the right and Bisnu judged the distance to be anything from a hundred to two hundred yards. He hesitated on the path, wondering what to do. Then he picked the kid up in his arms and hurried on in the direction of home and safety.

The panther called again, much closer now. If it was an ordinary panther, it would go away on finding that the kid was with Bisnu. If it was the man-eater, it would not hesitate to attack the boy, for no man-eater fears a human. There was no time to lose and there did not seem much point in running. Bisnu looked up and down the hillside. The forest was far behind him and there were only a few trees in his vicinity. He chose a spruce.

The branches of the Himalayan spruce are very

brittle and snap easily beneath a heavy weight. They were strong enough to support Bisnu's light frame. It was unlikely they would take the weight of a full-grown panther. At least that was what Bisnu hoped.

Holding the kid with one arm, Bisnu gripped a low branch and swung himself up into the tree. He was a good climber. Slowly but confidently he climbed halfway up the tree, until he was about twelve feet above the ground. He couldn't go any higher without risking a fall.

He had barely settled himself in the crook of a branch when the panther came into the open, running into the clearing at a brisk trot. This was no stealthy approach, no wary stalking of its prey. It was the man-eater, all right. Bisnu felt a cold shiver run down his spine. He felt a little sick.

The panther stood in the clearing with a slight thrusting forward of the head. This gave it the appearance of gazing intently and rather short-sightedly at some invisible object in the clearing. But there is nothing short-sighted about a panther's vision. Its sight and hearing are acute.

Bisnu remained motionless in the tree and sent up a prayer to all the gods he could think of. But the kid began bleating. The panther looked up and gave its deep-throated, rasping grunt—a fearsome sound, calculated to strike terror in any tree-borne animal. Many a monkey, petrified by a panther's roar, has fallen from its perch to make a meal for Mr Spots. The man-eater was trying the same technique on Bisnu. But though the boy was trembling with fright, he clung firmly to the trunk of the spruce tree.

The panther did not make any attempt to leap into the tree. Perhaps, it knew instinctively that this was not the type of tree that it could climb. Instead, it described a semicircle around the tree, keeping its face turned towards Bisnu. Then it disappeared into the bushes.

The man-eater was cunning. It hoped to put the boy off his guard, perhaps entice him down from the tree. For, a few seconds later, with a half-pitched growl, it rushed back into the clearing and then stopped, staring up at the boy in some surprise. The panther was getting frustrated. It snarled, and putting its forefeet up against the tree trunk, began scratching at the bark in the manner of an ordinary domestic cat. The tree shook at each thud of the beast's paw.

Bisnu began shouting for help.

The moon had not yet come up. Down in Manjari village, Bisnu's mother and sister stood in their lighted doorway, gazing anxiously up the pathway. Every now and then, Puja would turn to take a look at the small clock.

Sanjay's father appeared in a field below. He had a kerosene lantern in his hand.

'Sister, isn't your boy home as yet?' he asked.

'No, he hasn't arrived. We are very worried. He should have been home an hour ago. Do you think the panther will be about tonight? There's going to be a moon.'

'True, but it won't be dark for another hour. I will fetch the other menfolk and we will go up the mountain for your boy. There may have been a landslide during the rain. Perhaps the path has been washed away.'

'Thank you, brother. But arm yourselves, just in case the panther is about.'

'I will take my spear,' said Kalam Singh. 'I have sworn to spear that devil when I find him. There is some evil spirit dwelling in the beast and it must be destroyed!'

'I am coming with you,' said Puja.

'No, you cannot go,' said her mother. 'It's bad enough that Bisnu is in danger. You stay at home with me. This work is for men.'

'I shall be safe with them,' insisted Puja. 'I am going, Mother!'

And she jumped down the embankment into the field and followed Sanjay's father through the village.

Ten minutes later, two men armed with axes had joined Kalam Singh in the courtyard of his house and the small party moved silently and swiftly up the mountain path. Puja walked in the middle of the group, holding the lantern. As soon as the village lights were hidden by a shoulder of the hill, the men began to shout— both to frighten the panther, if it was about, and to give themselves courage.

Bisnu's mother closed the front door and turned to the image of Ganesha for comfort and help.

Bisnu's calls were carried on the wind and Puja and the men heard him while they were still half a mile away. Their own shouts increased in volume and, hearing their voices, Bisnu felt strength return to his shaking limbs. Emboldened by the approach of his own people, he began shouting insults at the snarling panther, then throwing twigs and small branches at the enraged animal. The kid added its bleats to the boy's shouts, the birds took up the chorus. The langurs squealed and grunted, the searchers shouted themselves hoarse and the panther howled with rage. The forest had never before been so noisy.

As the search party drew near, they could hear the panther's savage snarls, and hurried, fearing that perhaps Bisnu had been seized. Puja began to run.

'Don't rush ahead, girl,' said Kalam Singh. 'Stay between us.'

The panther, now aware of the approaching humans, stood still in the middle of the clearing, head thrust forward in a familiar stance. There seemed too many men for one panther. When the animal saw the light of the lantern dancing between the trees, it turned, snarled defiance and hate, and without another look at the boy in the tree, disappeared into the bushes. It was not yet ready for a showdown.

VII

Nobody turned up to claim the little goat, so Bisnu kept it. A goat was a poor substitute for a dog, but, like Mary's lamb, it followed Bisnu wherever he went, and the boy couldn't help being touched by its devotion. He took it down to the stream, where it would skip about in the shallows and nibble the sweet grass that grew on the banks.

As for the panther, frustrated in its attempt on Bisnu's life, it did not wait long before attacking another human.

It was Chittru who came running down the path one

afternoon, bubbling excitedly about the panther and the postman.

Chittru, deeming it safe to gather ripe bilberries in the daytime, had walked about half a mile up the path from the village, when he had stumbled across Mela Ram's mailbag lying on the ground. Of the postman himself there was no sign. But a trail of blood led through the bushes.

Once again, a party of men headed by Kalam Singh and accompanied by Bisnu and Chittru, went out to look for the postman. But though they found Mela Ram's bloodstained clothes, they could not find his body. The panther had made no mistake this time.

It was to be several weeks before Manjari had a new postman.

A few days after Mela Ram's disappearance, an old woman was sleeping with her head near the open door of her house. She had been advised to sleep inside with the door closed but the nights were hot and anyway the old woman was a little deaf, and in the middle of the night, an hour before moonrise, the panther seized her by the throat. Her strangled cry woke her grown-up son, and all the men in the village woke up at his shouts and came running.

The panther dragged the old woman out of the house and down the steps, but left her when the men approached with their axes and spears, and made off into the bushes. The old woman was still alive and the men made a rough stretcher of bamboo and vines and started carrying her up the path. But they had not gone far when she began to cough, and because of her terrible throat wounds, her lungs collapsed and she died.

It was the 'dark of the month'—the week of the new moon when nights are darkest.

Bisnu, closing the front door and lighting the kerosene lantern, said, 'I wonder where that panther is tonight!'

The panther was busy in another village: Sarru's village.

A woman and her daughter had been out in the evening bedding the cattle down in the stable. The girl had gone into the house and the woman was following. As she bent down to go in at the low door, the panther sprang from the bushes. Fortunately, one of its paws hit the doorpost and broke the force of the attack, or the woman would have been killed. When she cried out, the men came around shouting and the panther slunk off. The woman had deep scratches on her back and was badly shocked.

The next day, a small party of villagers presented themselves in front of the magistrate's office at Kempty and demanded that something be done about the panther. But the magistrate was away on tour and there was no one else in Kempty who had a gun. Mr Nautiyal met the villagers and promised to write to a well-known shikari but said that it would be at least a fortnight before the shikari would be able to come.

Bisnu was fretting because he could not go to school. Most boys would be only too happy to miss school, but when you are living in a remote village in the mountains, and having an education is the only way of seeing the world, you look forward to going to school, even if it is five miles from home. Bisnu's exams were only two weeks away and he didn't want to remain in the same class while the others were promoted. Besides, he knew he could pass even though he had missed a number of lessons. But he had to sit for the exams. He couldn't miss them.

'Cheer up, Brother,' said Puja, as they sat drinking glasses of hot tea after their evening meal. 'The panther may go away once the rains break.'

'Even the rains are late this year,' said Bisnu. 'It's so hot and dry. Can't we open the door?'

'And be dragged down the steps by the panther?' said his mother. 'It isn't safe to have the window open, let alone the door.'

And she went to the small window—through which a cat would have found difficulty in passing—and bolted it firmly.

With a sigh of resignation, Bisnu threw off all his clothes except his underwear and stretched himself out on the earthen floor.

'We will be rid of the beast soon,' said his mother. 'I know it in my heart. Our prayers will be heard, and you shall go to school and pass your exams.'

To cheer up her children, she told them a humorous story which had been handed down to her by her grandmother. It was all about a tiger, a panther, and a bear, the three of whom were made to feel very foolish by a thief hiding in the hollow trunk of a banyan tree. Bisnu was sleepy and did not listen very attentively. He dropped off to sleep before the story was finished.

When he woke, it was dark and his mother and sister were asleep on the cot. He wondered what it was that had woken him. He could hear his sister's easy breathing and the steady ticking of the clock. Far away, an owl hooted—an unlucky sign, his mother would have said; but she was asleep and Bisnu was not superstitious.

And then he heard something scratching at the door, and the hair on his head felt tight and prickly. It was like a cat scratching, only louder. The door creaked a little whenever it felt the impact of the paw—a heavy paw, as Bisnu could tell from the dull sound it made.

'It's the panther,' he muttered under his breath, sitting up on the hard floor.

The door, he felt, was strong enough to resist the panther's weight. And if he set up an alarm, he could rouse the village. But the middle of the night was no time for the bravest of men to tackle a panther.

In a corner of the room stood a long bamboo stick with a sharp knife tied to one end, which Bisnu sometimes used for spearing fish. Crawling on all fours across the room, he grasped the homemade spear, and then scrambling on to a cupboard, he drew level with the skylight window. He could get his head and shoulders through the window.

'What are you doing up there?' said Puja, who had woken up at the sound of Bisnu shuffling about the room.

'Be quiet,' said Bisnu. 'You'll wake Mother.'

Their mother was awake by now. 'Come down from there, Bisnu. I can hear a noise outside.'

'Don't worry,' said Bisnu, who found himself looking

down on the wriggling animal which was trying to get its paw in under the door. With his mother and Puja awake, there was no time to lose.

He had got the spear through the window, and though he could not manoeuvre it so as to strike the panther's head, he brought the sharp end down with considerable force on the animal's rump.

With a roar of pain and rage the man-eater leapt down from the steps and disappeared into the darkness. It did not pause to see what had struck it. Certain that no human could have come upon it in that fashion, it ran fearfully to its lair, howling until the pain subsided.

VIII

A panther is an enigma. There are occasions when it proves itself to be the most cunning animal under the sun and yet the very next day it will walk into an obvious trap that no self-respecting jackal would ever go near. One day a panther will prove itself to be a complete coward and run like a hare from a couple of dogs, and the very next it will dash in amongst half a dozen men sitting around a campfire and inflict terrible injuries on them.

It is not often that a panther is taken by surprise, as its power of sight and hearing are very acute. It is a master at the art of camouflage and its spotted coat is admirably suited for the purpose. It does not need heavy jungle to hide in. A couple of bushes and the light and shade from surrounding trees are enough to make it almost invisible.

Because the Manjari panther had been fooled by Bisnu, it did not mean that it was a stupid panther. It simply meant that it had been a little careless. And Bisnu and Puja, growing in confidence since their midnight encounter with the animal, became a little careless themselves.

Puja was hoeing the last field above the house and Bisnu, at the other end of the same field, was chopping up several branches of green oak, prior to leaving the wood to dry in the loft. It was late afternoon and the descending sun glinted in patches on the small river. It was a time of day when only the most desperate and daring of man-eaters would be likely to show itself.

Pausing for a moment to wipe the sweat from his brow, Bisnu glanced up at the hillside and his eye caught sight of a rock on the brow of the hill which seemed unfamiliar to him. Just as he was about to look elsewhere, the round rock began to grow and then alter its shape, and Bisnu watching in fascination was at last able to make out the head and forequarters of the panther. It looked enormous from the angle at which he saw it and for a moment he thought it was a tiger. But Bisnu knew instinctively that it was the man-eater.

Slowly, the wary beast pulled itself to its feet and began to walk around the side of the great rock. For a second it disappeared and Bisnu wondered if it had gone away. Then it reappeared and the boy was all excitement again. Very slowly and silently the panther walked across the face of the rock until it was in direct line with the corner of the field where Puja was working.

With a thrill of horror Bisnu realized that the panther

was stalking his sister. He shook himself free from the spell which had woven itself around him and shouting hoarsely ran forward.

'Run, Puja, run!' he called. 'It's on the hill above you!'

Puja turned to see what Bisnu was shouting about. She saw him gesticulate to the hill behind her, looked up just in time to see the panther crouching for his spring.

With great presence of mind, she leapt down the banking of the field and tumbled into an irrigation ditch.

The springing panther missed its prey, lost its foothold on the slippery shale banking, and somersaulted into the ditch a few feet away from Puja. Before the animal could recover from its surprise, Bisnu was dashing down the slope, swinging his axe and shouting, 'Maro, maro!'

Two men came running across the field. They, too, were armed with axes. Together with Bisnu they made a half-circle around the snarling animal, which turned at bay and plunged at them in order to get away. Puja wriggled along the ditch on her stomach. The men aimed their axes at the panther's head and Bisnu had the satisfaction of getting in a well-aimed blow between the eyes. The animal then charged straight at one of the men, knocked him over and tried to get at his throat. Just then Sanjay's father arrived with his long spear. He plunged the end of the spear into the panther's neck.

The panther left its victim and ran into the bushes, dragging the spear through the grass and leaving a trail of blood on the ground.

The men followed cautiously—all except the man who had been wounded, and who lay on the ground, while

Puja and the other womenfolk rushed up to help him.

The panther had made for the bed of the stream and Bisnu, Sanjay's father, and their companions were able to follow it quite easily. The water was red where the panther had crossed the stream and the rocks were stained with blood. After they had gone downstream for about a furlong, they found the panther lying still on its side at the edge of the water. It was mortally wounded but it continued to wave its tail like an angry cat. Then, even the tail lay still.

'It is dead,' said Bisnu. 'It will not trouble us again in this body.'

'Let us be certain,' said Sanjay's father and he bent down and pulled the panther's tail.

There was no response.

'It is dead,' said Kalam Singh. 'No panther would suffer such an insult were it alive!'

They cut down a long piece of thick bamboo and tied the panther to it by its feet. Then, with their enemy hanging upside down from the bamboo pole, they started back for the village.

'There will be a feast at my house tonight,' said Kalam Singh. 'Everyone in the village must come. And tomorrow we will visit all the villages in the valley and show them the dead panther, so that they may move about again without fear.'

'We can sell the skin in Kempty,' said their companion. 'It will fetch a good price.'

'But the claws we will give to Bisnu,' said Kalam Singh, putting his arm around the boy's shoulders. 'He has done a man's work today. He deserves the claws.'

A panther's or tiger's claws are considered to be lucky charms.

'I will take only three claws,' said Bisnu. 'One each for my mother and sister, and one for myself. You may give the others to Sanjay and Chittru and the smaller children.'

As the sun set, a big fire was lit in the middle of the village of Manjari and the people gathered around it, singing and laughing. Kalam Singh killed his fattest goat and there was meat for everyone.

IX

Bisnu was on his way home. He had just handed in his first paper, arithmetic, which he had found quite easy. Tomorrow it would be algebra, and when he got home he would have to practise square roots and cube roots and fractional coefficients.

Mr Nautiyal and the entire class had been happy that he had been able to sit for the exams. He was also a hero to them for his part in killing the panther. The story had spread through the villages with the rapidity of a forest fire, a fire which was now raging in Kempty town.

When he walked past the hospital, he was whistling cheerfully.

Dr Taylor waved to him from the veranda steps.

'How is Sanjay now?' she asked.

'He is well,' said Bisnu.

'And your mother and sister?'

'They are well,' said Bisnu.

'Are you going to get yourself a new dog?'

'I am thinking about it,' said Bisnu. 'At present I have a baby goat—I am teaching it to swim!'

He started down the path to the valley. Dark clouds had gathered and there was a rumble of thunder. A storm was imminent.

'Wait for me!' shouted Sarru, running down the path behind Bisnu, his milk pails clanging against each other. He fell into step beside Bisnu.

'Well, I hope we don't have any more man-eaters for some time,' he said. 'I've lost a lot of money by not being able to take milk up to Kempty.'

'We should be safe as long as a shikari doesn't wound another panther. There was an old bullet wound in the man-eater's thigh. That's why it couldn't hunt in the forest. The deer were too fast for it.'

'Is there a new postman yet?'

'He starts tomorrow. A cousin of Mela Ram's.'

When they reached the parting of their ways, it had begun to rain a little.

'I must hurry,' said Sarru. It's going to get heavier any minute.'

'I feel like getting wet,' said Bisnu. 'This time it's the monsoon, I'm sure.'

Bisnu entered the forest on his own and at the same time the rain came down in heavy, opaque sheets. The trees shook in the wind and the langurs chattered with excitement.

It was still pouring when Bisnu emerged from the forest, drenched to the skin. But the rain stopped suddenly, just as the village of Manjari came into view.

The sun appeared through a rift in the clouds. The leaves and the grass gave out a sweet, fresh smell.

Bisnu could see his mother and sister in the field transplanting the rice seedlings. The menfolk were driving the yoked oxen through the thin mud of the fields while the children hung on to the oxen's tails, standing on the plain wooden harrows, and with weird cries and shouts sending the animals almost at a gallop along the narrow terraces.

Bisnu felt the urge to be with them, working in the fields. He ran down the path, his feet falling softly on the wet earth. Puja saw him coming and waved at him. She met him at the edge of the field.

'How did you find your paper today?' she asked.

'Oh, it was easy.' Bisnu slipped his hand into hers and together they walked across the field. Puja felt something smooth and hard against her fingers and, before she could see what Bisnu was doing, he had slipped a pair of bangles on her wrist.

'I remembered,' he said with a sense of achievement.

Puja looked at the bangles and blurted out: 'But they are blue, Bhai, and I wanted red and gold bangles!' And then, when she saw him looking crestfallen, she hurried on: 'But they are very pretty and you did remember.... Actually, they are just as nice as red and gold bangles! Come into the house when you are ready. I have made something special for you.'

'I am coming,' said Bisnu, turning towards the house. 'You don't know how hungry a man gets, walking five miles to reach home!'

THE LAST TIGER

On the left bank of the Ganga, where it emerges from the Himalayan foothills, there is a long stretch of heavy forest. There are villages on the fringe of the forest, inhabited by bamboo cutters and farmers, but there are few signs of commerce or religion. Hunters, however, have found it an ideal hunting ground over the last seventy years, and as a result the animals are not as numerous as they used to be. The trees, too, have been disappearing slowly; and, as the forest recedes, the animals lose their food and shelter and move on, further into the foothills. Slowly, they are being denied the right to live.

Only the elephants could cross the river. And two years ago, when a large area of forest was cleared to make way for a refugee resettlement camp, a herd of elephants—finding their favourite food, the green shoots of the bamboo, in short supply—waded across the river. They crashed through the suburbs of Haridwar, knocked down a factory wall, plucked away several tin roofs, held up a train, and left a trail of devastation in their wake until they reached a new forest, still untouched, where they settled down to a new life—but an unsettled, wary life. They did not know when men would appear again, with tractors and bulldozers and dynamite.

There was a time when this forest provided food and shelter for some thirty or forty tigers; but men in search of trophies shot them all, and today there remains only one old tiger in the jungle. Many hunters have tried to get him. But he is a wise and crafty old tiger who knows the ways of men, and he has so far survived all attempts on his life.

This is his story. It is also the story of the jungle.

∽

Although the tiger has passed the prime of his life, he has lost none of his majesty; his muscles ripple beneath the golden yellow of his coat, and he walks through the long grass with the confidence of one who knows that he is still king, even though his subjects are fewer. His great head pushes through the foliage, and it is only his tail, swinging high, that shows occasionally above the sea of grass.

He is heading for water, the only water in the forest (if you don't count the river, which is several miles away)—the water of a large jheel, which is almost a lake during the rainy season, but just a muddy marsh at this time of the year, in the late spring.

Here, at different times of the day and night, all the animals come to drink—the long-horned sambar deer, the delicate spotted chital, the swamp deer, the wolves and jackals, the wild boar, the panthers—and the tiger. Since the elephants have gone, the water is usually clear except when buffaloes from the nearest village come to wallow, and then it is very muddy. These buffaloes, though they are not wild, are not afraid of the panther or even of the tiger. They know the panther is afraid of their long horns and they know the tiger prefers the flesh of the deer.

Today, there are several sambar at the water's edge, but they do not stay long. The tiger is coming with the breeze, and there is no mistaking its strong feline odour. The deer hold their heads high for a few moments, their nostrils twitching, and then scatter into the forest, disappearing behind screens of leaf and bamboo.

When the tiger arrives, there is no other animal near the water. But the birds are still there. The egrets continue to wade in the shallows, and a kingfisher darts low over the water, dives suddenly, a flash of blue and gold, and makes off with a slim silver fish, which glistens in the sun like a polished gem. A long brown snake glides amongst the water lilies and disappears beneath a fallen tree which lies rotting in the shallows.

The tiger waits in the shelter of a rock, his ears pricked up for the least unfamiliar sound; for he knows that it is often at this place that men lie up for him with guns; for they covet his beauty—they covet his stripes, and the gold of his body, and his fine teeth and his whiskers and his noble head. They would like to hang his pelt on a wall, and stick glass eyes in his head, and boast of their conquest over the king of the jungle.

The old tiger has been hunted before, and he does not usually show himself in the open during the day, but of late he has heard no guns, and if there were hunters around, you would have heard their guns (for a man with a gun cannot resist letting it off, even if it is only at a rabbit—or at another man). And, besides, the tiger is thirsty.

He is also feeling quite hot. It is March, and the shimmering dust-haze of summer has come early this year. Tigers—unlike other cats—are fond of water, and on a hot day will wallow for hours.

He walks into the water, in amongst the water lilies, and drinks slowly. He is seldom in a hurry when he eats or drinks. Other animals might bolt their food, but they are only other animals. A tiger has his dignity to preserve!

He raises his head and listens. One paw remains suspended in the air. A strange sound has come to him on the breeze, and he is wary of strange sounds. So he moves swiftly through the grass that borders the jheel, and climbs a hillock until he reaches his favourite rock. This rock is big enough to hide him and to give him shade. Anyone looking up from the jheel might think it strange that the rock has a round bump on the top. The bump is the tiger's head. He keeps it very still.

The sound he has heard is only the sound of a flute, sounding thin and reedy in the forest. It belongs to a boy, a slim brown boy who rides a buffalo. The boy blows vigorously on the flute, while another, slightly smaller boy, riding another buffalo, brings up the rear of the herd.

There are about eight buffaloes in the herd, and they belong to the families of Ramu and Shyam, the two Gujjar boys who are friends. The Gujjars are a caste who possess herds of buffaloes and earn their livelihood from the sale of milk and butter. The boys are about twelve years old, but they cannot tell you how many months past twelve, because in their village nobody thinks birthdays are important. They are almost the same age as the tiger, but he is old and experienced while they are still cubs.

∽

The tiger has often seen them at the tank, and he is not worried. He knows the village people will bring him no harm as long as he leaves their buffaloes alone. Once, when he was younger and full of bravado, he had killed a buffalo—not because he was hungry but because he was young and wanted to test his strength—and after that the villagers had hunted him for days, with spears, bows and arrows, and an old muzzle-loader. Now he left the buffaloes alone, even though the deer in the forest were not as numerous as before.

The boys know that a tiger lives in the jungle, for they have often heard him roar, but they do not know that today he is so near to them.

The tiger gazes down from his rock, and the sight of eight fat black buffaloes does make him give a low, throaty moan. But the boys are there, and besides—a buffalo is not easy to kill.

He decides to move on and find a cool shady place in the heart of the jungle, where he can rest during the warm afternoon and be free of the flies and mosquitoes that swarm around in the vicinity of the tank. At night he will hunt.

With a lazy, half-humorous roar—'A—oonh!'—he gets up from his haunches and saunters off into the jungle.

Even the gentlest of a tiger's roars can be heard half a mile away, and the boys, who are barely fifty yards off, look up immediately.

'There he goes!' calls Ramu, taking the flute from his lips and pointing with it towards the hillock. He is not afraid, for he knows that an un-hunted and uninjured tiger is not aggressive. 'Did you see him?'

'I saw his tail, just before he disappeared. He's a big tiger!'

'Do not call him tiger. Call him Uncle, or Maharaj.'

'Oh, why?'

'Don't you know that it's unlucky to call a tiger a tiger? My father always told me so. But if you meet a tiger, and call him Uncle, he will leave you alone.'

'I'll try and remember that,' says Shyam.

∽

The buffaloes are now well into the water, and some of them are lying down in the mud. Buffaloes love soft, wet mud and will wallow in it for hours. The more mud the better. Ramu, to avoid being dragged down into the mud with his buffalo, slips off its back and plunges into the water. Using an easy breaststroke, he swims across to a small islet covered with reeds and water lilies. Shyam is close behind him.

They lie down on their hard, flat stomachs on a patch of grass and allow the warm sun to beat down on their bare, brown bodies. Ramu is the more knowledgeable boy, because he has been to Haridwar several times with his father. Shyam has never been out of the village.

Shyam says, 'The pool is not so deep this year.'

'We have had no rain since January,' says Ramu. 'If we do not get rain soon, the tank may dry up altogether.'

'And then what will we do?'

'We? There is a well in the village. But even that may dry up. My father told me that it dried up once, just about the time I was born, and everyone had to walk ten miles to the river for water.'

'And what about the animals?'

'Some will stay here and die. Others will go to the river.

'But there are too many people near the river now— not only temples, but houses and factories—and the animals stay away. And the trees have been cut, so that between the jungle and the river there is no place to hide. Animals are afraid of the open—they are afraid of men with guns.'

'Even at night?'

'At night men come in jeeps, with searchlights. They kill the deer for meat, and sell the skins of tigers and panthers.'

'I didn't know a tiger's skin was worth anything.'

'It is worth more than our skins,' says Ramu knowingly. 'It will fetch six hundred rupees. Who would pay that much for our skins?'

'Our fathers would.'

'True—if they had the money.'

'If my father sold his fields, he would get more than six hundred rupees.'

'True—but if he sold his fields, none of you would have anything to eat. A man needs land as much as a tiger needs a jungle.'

'True,' says Shyam. 'And that reminds me—my mother asked me to take some roots home.'

'I will help you.'

They wade into the jheel until the water is up to their waists, and begin pulling up water lilies by the root. The flower is beautiful but the villagers value the root more. When cooked, it makes for a delicious and nourishing dish. The plant multiplies rapidly and is always in good supply. In the year when famine hit the village, it was only the root of the water lily that saved many from starvation.

When Shyam and Ramu have finished gathering roots, they emerge from the water and spend some time wrestling with each other, slipping about in the soft mud which soon covers them from head to toe.

To get rid of the mud, they dive into the water again and swim across to their buffaloes. Then, digging their heels into the thick hides of the buffaloes, the boys race them across the jheel, shouting and hollering so much that all the birds fly away in disgust, and the monkeys set up a shrill chattering of their own in the dhak trees.

In March, the twisted, leafless flame of the forest or dhak trees are ablaze with flaming scarlet and orange flowers.

It is evening, and the twilight is fading fast, when the buffalo herd finally wends its way homewards, to be greeted outside the village by the barking of dogs, the gurgle of hookah pipes, and the homely smell of cowdung smoke.

◯

The tiger makes a kill that night. He approaches with the wind against him, and the unsuspecting spotted deer does not see him until it is too late. A blow on the deer's haunches from the tiger's paw brings it down, and then the great beast fastens on to the struggling deer's throat. It is all over in a few minutes. The tiger is too quick and strong, and the deer does not struggle for long.

The deer's life is over, but he has not lived in fear of death. It is only man's imagination and fear of the hereafter that makes him afraid of meeting death. In the jungle, sudden death appears at intervals. Wild creatures do not have to think about it, and so the sudden passing of one of their number due to the arrival of some flesh-eating animal is only a fleeting incident soon forgotten by the survivors.

The tiger feasts well, growling with pleasure as he eats, and then leaves the carcass in the jungle for the vultures and jackals. The old tiger never returns to the same deer's carcass, even if there is still some flesh on it. In the past, when he has done that, he has often found a man sitting in a tree over the kill, waiting for him with a rifle.

His belly full, the tiger comes to the edge of the forest, looks out across the wasteland out over the deep, singing river, at the twinkling lights of Haridwar on the opposite bank, and raises his head and roars his defiance at the world.

He is a lonesome bachelor. It is five or six years since he had a mate. She was shot by trophy-hunters, and the cubs, two of them, were trapped by men who trade in wild animals: one went to a circus, where it had to learn undignified tricks and respond to the flick of a whip, the other, more fortunate, went first to a zoo in Delhi and was later transferred to a zoo in America.

Sometimes, when the old tiger is very lonely, he gives a great roar, which can be heard throughout the forest. The villagers think he is roaring in anger, but the animals know that he is really roaring out of loneliness. When the sound of his roar has died away, he pauses, standing still, waiting for an answering roar, but it never comes. It is taken up instead by the shrill scream of a barbet high up in a sal tree.

It is dawn now, dew-fresh and cool, and the jungle dwellers are on the move. The black, beady little eyes of a jungle rat were fixed on a small brown hen who was returning cautiously to her nest. He had a large family to feed, and he knew that in the hen's nest was a clutch of delicious fawn-coloured eggs. He waited patiently for nearly an hour before he had the satisfaction of seeing the hen leave her nest and go off in search of food.

As soon as she had gone, the rat lost no time in making his raid. Slipping quietly out of his hole, he slithered along among the leaves, but, clever as he was, he did not realize that his own movements were being watched.

A pair of grey mongooses were scouting about in the dry grass. They, too, were hungry, and eggs usually figured large on their menu. Now, lying still on an outcrop of rock, they watched the rat sneaking along, occasionally sniffing at the air, and finally vanishing behind a boulder. When he reappeared, he was struggling to roll an egg uphill towards his hole.

The rat was in great difficulty, pushing the egg sometimes with his paws, sometimes with his nose. The ground was rough, and the egg wouldn't go straight. Deciding that he must have help, he scuttled off to call his spouse. Even now the mongoose did not descend on that tantalizing egg. He waited until the rat returned with his wife, and then watched as the male rat took the egg firmly between his forepaws and rolled over on to his back. The female rat then grabbed her mate's tail and began to drag him along.

Totally absorbed in their struggle with the egg, the rats did not hear the mongooses approaching. When these two large furry visitors suddenly bobbed up from behind a stone, the rats squealed with fright, abandoned the egg, and fled for their lives.

The mongooses wasted no time in breaking open the egg and making a meal of it. But just as, a few minutes ago, the rat had not noticed their approach, so now they did not notice the village boy, carrying a small bright axe and a net bag in his hands, creeping along.

Ramu too was searching for eggs, and when he saw the mongooses busy with one, he stood still to watch them, his eyes roving in search of the nest. He was hoping the mongooses would lead him to the nest, but, when they had finished their meal, the breeze took them in another direction, and Ramu had to do his own searching. He failed to find the nest, and moved further into the forest. The rat's hopes were just reviving when, to his disgust, the mother hen returned.

Ramu now made his way to a mahua tree.

The flowers of the mahua tree can be eaten by animals as well as men. Bears are particularly fond of them and will eat large quantities of its flowers which gradually start fermenting in their stomachs with the result that the animals get quite drunk. Ramu had often seen a couple of bears stumbling home to their cave, bumping into each other or into the trunks of trees—they are short-sighted to begin with, and when drunk can hardly see at all—but their sense of smell and hearing are so good that they finally find their way home.

Ramu decided he would gather some mahua flowers, and climbed swiftly on to the tree, which is leafless when it blossoms. He began plucking the white flowers and throwing them to the ground. He had been in the tree for about five minutes when he heard the whining grumble of a bear, and presently a young sloth bear ambled into the clearing beneath the tree.

He was a small bear, little more than a cub, and Ramu was not frightened, but, because he thought the mother might be in the vicinity, he decided to take no chances, and sat very still, waiting to see what the bear would do. He hoped it wouldn't choose the same mahua tree for a meal.

At first the young bear put his nose to the ground and sniffed his way along until he came to a large white anthill. Here he began huffing and puffing, blowing rapidly in and out of his nostrils, so that the dust from the anthill flew in all directions. But he was a disappointed bear, because the anthill had been deserted long ago. And so, grumbling, he made his way across to a wild plum—a tall tree, the wild plum—and shinning rapidly up the smooth trunk, was soon perched on its topmost branches. It was only then that he saw Ramu.

The bear at once scrambled several feet higher up the tree, and laid himself out flat on a branch. It wasn't a very thick branch and left a large expanse of bear showing on either side of it. The bear tucked his head away behind another branch, and, so long as he could not see Ramu, seemed quite satisfied that he was well hidden, though he couldn't help grumbling with anxiety, for a bear, like most animals, is afraid of man—until he discovers that man is afraid of him.

Bears, however, are also very curious—and curiosity has often led them into trouble. Slowly, inch by inch, the young bear's black snout appeared over the edge of the branch, but immediately, the eyes came into view and met Ramu's. He drew back with a jerk and the head was once more hidden. The bear did this two or three times, and Ramu, highly amused, waited until it wasn't looking, then moved some way down the tree. When the bear looked up again and saw that the boy was missing, he was so pleased with himself that he stretched right across to the next branch, to get at a plum. Ramu chose this moment to burst into loud laughter. The startled bear tumbled out of the tree, dropped through the branches for a distance of some fifteen feet, and landed with a thud in a heap of dry leaves.

And then several things happened almost at the same time.

The mother bear came charging into the clearing. Spotting Ramu in the tree, she reared up on her hind legs, grunting fiercely. It was Ramu's turn to be startled. There are few animals as dangerous as a rampaging mother bear, and the boy knew that one blow from her clawed forepaws could rip his skull open.

But before the bear could approach the tree, there was a tremendous roar, and the tiger bounded into the clearing. He had been asleep in the bushes not far away—he liked a good sleep after a heavy meal—and the noise in the clearing had woken him.

He was in a very bad temper, and his loud 'A—oonh!' made his displeasure quite clear. The bears turned and ran from the clearing, the youngster squealing with fright.

The tiger then came into the centre of the clearing, looked up at the trembling boy, and roared again.

Ramu nearly fell out of the tree.

'Good day to you, Uncle,' he stammered, showing his teeth in a nervous grin.

Perhaps this was too much for the tiger. With a low growl, he turned his back on the mahua tree and padded off into the jungle, his tail twitching in disgust.

∽

That night, when Ramu told his parents and grandfather about the tiger and how it had saved him from a female bear, a number of stories were told about tigers, some of whom had been gentlemen, others rogues. Sooner or later the conversation came round to man-eaters, and Grandfather told two stories, which he swore were true, though the others only half believed him.

The first story concerned the belief that a man-eating tiger is guided towards his next victim by the spirit of a human being previously killed and eaten by the tiger. Grandfather said that he actually knew three hunters who sat up in a machan over a human kill, and when the tiger came, the corpse sat up and pointed with his right hand at the men in the tree. The tiger then went away. But the hunters knew he would return, and one man was brave enough to get down from the tree and tie the right arm of the corpse to the body. Later, when the tiger returned, the corpse sat up and pointed out the men with his left hand. The enraged tiger sprang into the tree and killed his enemies in the machan.

'And then there was a bania,' said Grandfather, beginning another story, 'who lived in a village in the jungle. He wanted to visit a neighbouring village to collect some money that was owed him, but as the road lay through heavy forest, in which lived a terrible man-eating tiger, he did not know what to do. Finally, he went to a sadhu who gave him two powders. By eating the first powder, he could turn into a huge tiger, capable of dealing with any other tiger in the jungle, and by eating the second he could become a bania again.

'Armed with his two powders, and accompanied by his pretty young wife, the bania set out on his journey. They had not gone far into the forest when they came upon the man-eater sitting in the middle of the road. Before swallowing the first powder, the bania told his wife to stay where she was, so that when he returned after killing the tiger, she could at once give him the second powder and enable him to resume his old shape.

'Well, the bania's plan worked, but only up to a point. He swallowed the first powder and immediately became a magnificent tiger. With a great roar, he bounded towards the man-eater, and after a brief, furious fight, killed his opponent. Then, with his jaws still dripping blood, he returned to his wife.

'The poor girl was terrified and spilt the second powder on the ground. The bania was so angry that he pounced on his wife and killed and ate her. And afterwards this terrible tiger was so enraged at not being able to become a human again that he killed and ate hundreds of people all over the country.'

'The only people he spared,' said Grandfather, with a twinkle in his eye, 'were those who owed him money. A bania never gives up a loan as lost, and the tiger still hoped that one day he might become a human again and be able to collect his dues.'

Next morning, when Ramu came back from the well which was used to irrigate his father's fields, he found a crowd of curious children surrounding a jeep and three strangers with guns. Each of the strangers had a gun, and they were accompanied by two bearers and a vast amount of provisions.

They had heard that there was a tiger in the area, and they wanted to shoot it.

One of the hunters, who looked even stranger than the others, had come all the way to India for a tiger, and he had vowed that he would not leave the country without a tiger's skin in his baggage. One of his companions had said that he could buy a tiger's skin in Delhi, but the hunter did not like the idea and said he'd have nothing to do with a tiger that he hadn't shot.

These men had money to spend, and, as most of the villagers needed money badly, they were only too willing to construct a machan for the hunters. The platform, big enough to take the three men, was put up in the branches of a tall toon, or mahogany tree.

It was the only night the hunters used the machan. At the end of March, though the days are warm, the nights are still cold. The hunters had neglected to bring blankets, and by midnight their teeth were chattering. Ramu, having tied up a goat for them at the foot of the tree, made as if to go home but instead circled the area, hanging up bits and pieces of old clothing on small trees and bushes. He thought he owed that much to the tiger. He knew the wily old king of the jungle would keep well away from the goat if he thought there were humans in the vicinity. And where there are men's clothes, there will be men.

As soon as it was dark, the goat began bleating, loud enough for any self-respecting tiger to hear it, but perhaps the ruse was too obvious, or perhaps the clothes

Ramu had hung out were warning enough, because the tiger did not come near the toon tree. In any case, the men in the tree soon gave themselves away.

The cold was really too much for them. A flask of brandy was produced, and passed round, and it was not long before there was more purpose to finishing the brandy than to finishing off a tiger. Silent at first, the men soon began talking in whispers, and to jungle creatures a human whisper is as telling as a trumpet call. Soon the men were quite merry, talking in loud voices. And when the first morning light crept over the forest, and Ramu and his friends came by to see if the goat still lived, they found the hunters fast asleep in the machan.

The shikaris looked surly and embarrassed when they trudged back to the village.

'No game left in these parts,' said one.

'The wrong time of the year for tiger,' said another.

'I don't know what the country's coming to,' said the third.

And complaining about the weather, the quality of cartridges, the quality of rum, and the perversity of tigers, they drove away in disgust.

It was not until the onset of summer that an event occurred which altered the hunting habits of the tiger and brought him into conflict with the villagers.

∽

There had been no rain for almost two months, and the grass had become a dry yellow. Some refugee settlers, living in an area where the forest had been cleared, were careless in putting out a fire. The tiger sniffed the acrid smell of smoke in the air, and, wandering to the edge of the jungle, saw in the distance the dancing lights of a forest fire. As night came on, the flames grew more vivid, the smell stronger. The tiger turned and made for the jheel, where he knew he would be safe, provided he swam across to the little island in the centre.

Next morning he was on the island, which was untouched by the fire. But his surroundings had changed. The slopes of the hills were black with burnt grass, and most of the tall bamboo had disappeared. The deer and the wild pig, finding that their natural cover had gone, fled further east.

The tiger prowled throughout the smoking forest but he found no game. Once he came across the body of a burnt rabbit, but he could not eat it. He drank at the jheel and settled down in a shady spot to sleep the day away. Perhaps, by evening, some of the animals would return. If not, he too would have to look for new hunting grounds—or new game.

The tiger had not eaten for five days and he was so hungry that he had been forced to scratch about in the grass and leaves for worms and beetles. This was a sad comedown for the king of the jungle. But even now he hesitated to leave the area, for he had a deep suspicion and fear of the forests further south and east—forests that were fast being swallowed up by human habitation. He could have gone north, into the hills, but they did not provide him with the long grass he needed. A panther could manage quite well in the hills, but not a tiger who loved the natural privacy of heavy jungle. In the hills, he would have to hide all the time.

At break of day, the tiger came to the jheel. The water was now shallow and muddy, and a green scum had spread over the top. But the water was still drinkable, and the tiger had quenched his thirst.

He lay down across his favourite rock, hoping for a deer, but none approached. He was about to get up and go away when he heard the warning chatter of a lone langur. Some animal was definitely approaching.

The tiger at once dropped flat on the ground, his tawny skin merging with the dry grass. A heavy animal was moving through the bushes, and the tiger waited patiently until a buffalo emerged and came to the water. The buffalo was alone.

He was a big male buffalo, and his long, curved horns lay right back across his shoulders. He moved leisurely towards the water, completely unaware of the tiger's presence.

The tiger hesitated before making his charge. It was a long time—many years—since he had killed a buffalo, and he knew the villagers would not like it. But hunger helped him overcome his caution. There was no morning breeze, everything was still, and the smell of the tiger did not carry to the buffalo. The monkey still chattered in a nearby tree, but his warning went unheeded.

Moving at a crouch, the tiger skirted the edge of the jheel and approached the buffalo from the rear. The water birds, who were used to the presence of both animals, did not raise an alarm.

Getting closer, the tiger glanced around to see if there were men, or other buffaloes, in the vicinity. Then, satisfied that he was alone, he crept forward. The buffalo was drinking, standing in shallow water at the edge of the tank, when the tiger charged from the side and bit deep into the animal's thigh.

The buffalo turned to fight, but the tendons of his right hind leg had been snapped, and he could only stagger forward a few paces. But he was not afraid. He bellowed, and lowered his horns at the tiger, but the great cat was too fast and, circling the buffalo, bit into the other hind leg.

The buffalo crashed to the ground, both hind legs crippled, and then the tiger dashed in, using both tooth and claw, biting deep into the buffalo's throat until blood gushed out from the jugular vein.

The buffalo gave one long last bellow before dying.

The tiger, having rested, now began to gorge himself, but, even though he had been starving for days, he could not finish the buffalo. At least one good meal still remained when, satisfied and feeling his strength return, he quenched his thirst at the jheel. Then he dragged the remains of the buffalo into the bushes and went off to find a place to sleep. He would return to the kill when he was hungry.

The villagers were upset when they discovered that a buffalo was missing, and next day, when Ramu and Shyam came running home to say that they had found the carcass near the jheel, half-eaten by the tiger, the men were disturbed and angry. They felt that the tiger had tricked and deceived them. And they knew that once he found he could kill buffaloes quite easily, he would make a habit of it.

Kundan Singh, Shyam's father, and the owner of the dead buffalo, said he would go after the tiger himself.

'It is all very well to talk about what you will do to the tiger,' said his wife, 'but you should never have let the buffalo go off on its own.'

'He had been out on his own before,' said Kundan. 'This is the first time the tiger has attacked one of our beasts. A shaitan—a devil—has entered the Maharaj.'

'He must have been very hungry,' said Shyam.

'Well, we are hungry too,' said Kundan. 'Our best buffalo—the only male in our herd—'

'The tiger will kill again,' said Ramu's father.

'If we let him,' said Kundan. 'Should we send for the shikaris?'

'No. They were not clever. The tiger will escape them easily. And, besides, there is no time. The tiger will return for another meal tonight. We must finish him off ourselves!'

'But how?'

Kundan Singh smiled secretively, played with the ends of his moustache for a few moments, and then, with great pride, produced from under his cot a double-barrelled gun of ancient vintage.

'My father bought it from an Englishman,' he said.

'How long ago was that?'

'At the time I was born.'

'And have you ever used it?' asked Ramu's father,

who was not sure that the gun would work.

'Well, some years back, I let it off at some bandits. You remember the time when those dacoits raided our village? They chose the wrong village, and were severely beaten for their pains. As they left, I fired my gun off at them, and as a result they didn't stop running until they had crossed the Ganga!'

'Yes, but did you hit anyone?'

'I would have, if someone's goat hadn't got in the way at the last moment. But we had roast mutton that night! Don't worry, brother, I know how the thing works. It takes a fistful of powder and bullets the size of pigeon's eggs!'

Accompanied by Ramu's father and some others, Kundan set out for the jheel, where, without shifting the buffalo's carcass—for they knew the tiger would not come near them if it suspected a trap—they made another machan in a tall tree some thirty feet from the kill.

Later that evening—at the 'hour of cow-dust', Kundan Singh and Ramu's father settled down for the night on their crude tree platform.

Several hours passed, and nothing but a jackal was seen by the watchers. And then, just as the moon came up over the distant hills, Kundan and his companion were startled by a low 'A—oonh', followed by a suppressed, rumbling growl.

Kundan grasped his old gun, while his friend drew closer to him for comfort. There was complete silence for a minute or two—a time that was an agony of suspense for the watchers—and then there was the sound of a stealthy footfall on some dead leaves under the tree.

A moment later the tiger walked out into the moonlight and stood over his kill.

At first Kundan could do nothing. He was completely overawed by the size of this magnificent tiger. Ramu's father had to nudge him, and then Kundan quickly put the gun to his shoulder, aimed at the tiger's head, and pressed the trigger.

The gun went off with a flash and a tremendous roar, but the bullet only singed the tiger's shoulder.

The enraged animal rushed at the tree and tried to leap into its branches. Fortunately the machan had been built at a safe height, and the tiger, unable to reach it, roared twice, and then bounded off into the forest.

'What a tiger!' exclaimed Kundan, half in fear and half in admiration. 'I feel as though my liver has turned to water.'

'You missed him completely,' said Ramu's father. 'Your gun makes a big noise, but an arrow would have been more accurate.'

'I did not miss him,' said Kundan, feeling offended. 'You heard him roar, didn't you? He would not have been so angry if he had not been hit. If I have wounded him badly, he will die.'

'And if you have wounded him slightly, he may turn into a man-eater, and then where will we be?'

'I don't think he will come back,' said Kundan. 'He will leave these forests.'

They waited until the sun was up before coming

down from the tree. They found a few drops of blood on the dry grass, but no trail led into the forest, and Ramu's father was convinced that the wound was only a slight one.

The bullet, missing the fatal spot behind the ear, had only grazed the back of the skull and cut a deep groove at its base.

It took a few days to heal, and during this time the tiger lay low and did not go near the jheel except when it was very dark and he was very thirsty. The villagers thought the tiger had gone away, and Ramu and Shyam—accompanied by some other youths, and always carrying sticks and axes—began bringing the buffaloes to the tank again during the day; but they were careful not to let any of them stray far from the herd, and they returned home while it was still daylight.

While the buffaloes wallowed in the muddy water, and the boys wrestled on their grassy islet, a tawny eagle circled high above them, looking for a meal—a sure sign that some of the animals were beginning to return to the forest. It was not long before his keen eyes detected a movement in the glade below.

What the eagle saw was a baby hare, a small fluffy thing, its long pink-tinted ears laid flat along its sides. Had it not been creeping along between two large stones, it would have escaped notice. The eagle waited to see if the mother was about, and even as he waited he realized that he was not the only one who coveted this juicy hare. From the bushes there had appeared a sinuous yellow creature, pressed low to the ground and moving rapidly towards the hare. It was a yellow jungle cat, hardly noticeable in the scorched grass. With great stealth and artistry the jungle cat stalked the baby hare.

He pounced. The hare's squeal was cut short by the cat's cruel claws, but it had been heard by the mother hare, who now bounded into the glade and without the slightest hesitation attacked the surprised cat.

There was nothing haphazard about the hare's attack. She flashed around behind the cat and jumped clean over it. As she landed, she kicked back, sending a stinging jet of dust shooting into the cat's face. She did this again and again.

The bewildered cat, crouching and snarling, picked up the kill and tried to run away with it. But the hare would not permit this. She continued her leaping and buffeting till eventually the cat, out of sheer frustration, dropped the kill and attacked the mother.

The cat sprang at the hare a score of times lashing out with its claws, but the mother hare was both clever and agile enough to keep just out of reach of those terrible claws, and drew the cat further and further away from her baby—for she did not as yet know that it was dead.

The tawny eagle saw his chance. Swift and true, he swooped.

For a brief moment, as his wings overspread the furry little hare and his talons sank deep into it, he caught a glimpse of the cat racing towards him and the mother hare fleeing into the bushes. And then, with a shrill 'kee-ee-ee' of triumph, he rose and whirled away with his dinner.

The boys had heard this shrill cry and looked up just in time to see the eagle flying over the jheel with the small hare held firmly in its talons.

'Poor hare,' said Shyam. 'Its life was short.'

'That's the law of the jungle,' said Ramu. 'The eagle has a family too, and must feed it.'

'I wonder if we are any better than animals,' said Shyam.

'Perhaps we are a little better,' said Ramu. 'Grandfather always says, "To be able to laugh and to be merciful are the only things that make man better than beast".'

&

The next day, while the boys were taking the herd home, one of the buffaloes lagged behind. Ramu did not know the animal was missing until he heard her agonized bellow. He glanced over his shoulder just in time to see the big, striped tiger dragging the buffalo into a clump of young bamboo. At the same time the herd became aware of the danger, and the buffaloes snorted with fear as they hurried along the forest path. To urge them forward, and to warn his friends, Ramu cupped his hands to his mouth and gave vent to a yodelling call.

The buffaloes bellowed, the boys shouted, and the birds flew shrieking from the trees. It was almost a stampede by the time the herd emerged from the forest. The villagers heard the thunder of hoofs, and saw the herd coming home in dust and confusion, and knew that something was wrong. 'The tiger!' shouted Ramu. 'He is here! He has killed one of the buffaloes.'

'He is afraid of us no longer,' said Shyam.

'Did you see where he went?' asked Kundan Singh, hurrying up to them.

'I remember the place,' said Ramu. 'He dragged the buffalo in amongst the bamboo.'

'Then there is no time to lose,' said his father.

'Kundan, you take your gun and two men, and wait near the suspension bridge, where the Garur stream joins the Ganga. The jungle narrows there. We will beat the jungle from our side, and drive the tiger towards you. He will not escape us, unless he swims the river!'

'Good!' said Kundan, running into his house for his gun, with Shyam close at his heels. 'Was it one of our buffaloes again?' he asked.

'It was Ramu's buffalo this time,' said Shyam, 'A good milk buffalo.'

'Then Ramu's father will beat the jungle thoroughly. You boys had better come with me. It will not be safe for you to accompany the beaters.'

∽

And so, Kundan Singh carrying his gun and accompanied by Ramu, Shyam, and two men, headed for the river junction, while Ramu's father collected about twenty men from the village and, guided by one of the boys who had been with Ramu, made for the spot where the tiger had killed the buffalo.

The tiger was still eating when he heard the men coming. He had not expected to be disturbed so soon. With an angry 'Whoof!' he bounded into the bamboo thicket and watched the men through a screen of leaves and tall grass.

The men did not seem to take much notice of the dead buffalo, but gathered round their leader and held a consultation. Most of them carried hand drums which hung down to their waists by shoulder-straps. They also carried sticks, spears, and axes.

After a hurried conversation, they turned to face the jungle and began beating their drums with the palms of their hands.

Some of the men banged empty kerosene tins. These made even more noise than the drums.

The tiger did not like the noise and retreated further into the jungle. But he was surprised to find that the men, instead of going away, came after him into the jungle, banging away on their drums and tins, and shouting at the top of their voices. They had separated now, and advanced singly or in pairs, but nowhere were they more than fifteen yards apart. The tiger could easily have broken through this slowly advancing semicircle of men—one swift blow from his paw would have felled the strongest of them—but his main aim was to get away from the noise. He hated and feared the noise made by men.

He was not a man-eater and he would not attack a man unless he was very angry or very frightened or very desperate; and he was none of these things as yet. He had eaten well, and he would like to rest in peace—but there would be no rest for any animal until the men had gone with their tremendous clatter and din.

For an hour Ramu's father and the others beat the

jungle, calling, drumming, and trampling the undergrowth. The tiger had no rest. Whenever he was able to put some distance between himself and the men, he would sink down in some shady spot to rest, but, within five or ten minutes, the trampling and drumming would sound nearer, and the tiger, with an angry snarl, would get up and pad silently north along the narrowing strip of jungle, towards the junction of the Garur stream and the Ganga. Ten years back, he would have had jungle on his right in which to hide; but the trees had been felled long ago, to make way for more humans, and now he could only move to the left, towards the river.

It was about noon when the tiger finally appeared in the open. He longed for the darkness and security of the night, for the sun was his enemy. Kundan and the boys had a clear view of him as he stalked slowly along, now in the open with the sun glinting on his glossy side, now in the shade, or passing through the shorter reeds. He was still out of range of Kundan's gun, but there was no fear of his getting out of the beat, as the 'stops' were all picked by men from the village. He disappeared among some bushes but soon reappeared to retrace his steps, the beaters having done their work well. He was now only one hundred and fifty yards from the rocks where Kundan Singh waited, and he looked very big.

∽

The beat had closed in, and his exit along the bank downstream was completely blocked; so the tiger turned into a belt of reeds, and Kundan Singh expected that his head would soon peer out of the cover a few yards away. The beaters were now making a great noise, shouting and beating their drums, but nothing moved, and Ramu, watching from a distance, wondered, 'Has he slipped through the beaters?' And hoped he had.

Tins clashed, drums beat, and some of the men poked into the reeds with their spears or long bamboos. Perhaps one of these thrusts found a mark, because at last the tiger was roused, and with an angry, desperate snarl he charged out of the reeds, splashing his way through an inlet of mud and water.

Kundan Singh fired, and his bullet struck the tiger on the thigh.

The mighty animal stumbled; but he was up in a minute, and, rushing through a gap in the narrowing line of beaters, he made straight for the only way across the river—the suspension bridge that passed over the Ganga here, providing a route into the high hills beyond.

'We'll get him now,' said Kundan, priming his gun again. 'He's right in the open!'

The suspension bridge swayed and trembled as the wounded tiger lurched across it. Kundan fired, and this time the bullet hit the tiger on the shoulder. The animal bounded forward, lost his footing on the unfamiliar, slippery planks of the swaying bridge, and went over the side, falling headlong into the strong, swirling waters of the river.

He rose to the surface once, but the current took him under and away, and only a thin streak of blood remained on the river's surface.

Kundan and the others hurried downstream to see if the dead tiger had been washed up on the river's banks; but though they searched the riverside for several miles, they did not find the tiger. The river had taken him to its bosom. He had not provided anyone with a trophy. His skin would not be spread on a couch, nor would his head be hung upon a wall. No claw of his would be hung as a charm around the neck of a child. No villager would use his fat as a cure for rheumatism.

∽

At first the villagers were glad because they felt their buffaloes were safe. Then the men began to feel that something had gone out of their lives, out of the life of the forest; they began to feel that the forest was no longer a forest. It had been shrinking year after year, but, as long as the tiger had been there and the villagers had heard it roar at night, they had known that they were still secure from the intruders and newcomers who came to fell the trees and eat up the land and let the floodwaters into the village. But now that the tiger had gone, it was as though a protector had gone, leaving the forest open and vulnerable, easily destroyable. And, once the forest was destroyed, they too would be in danger....

There was another thing that had gone with the tiger, another thing that had been lost, a thing that was being lost everywhere—something called 'nobility'.

Ramu remembered something that his grandfather had once said, 'The tiger is the very soul of India, and when the last tiger has gone, so will the soul of the country.'

The boys lay flat on their stomachs on their little mud island and watched the monsoon clouds gathering overhead.

'The king of our forest is dead,' said Shyam. 'There are no more tigers.'

'There must be tigers,' said Ramu. 'How can there be an India without tigers?'

The river had carried the tiger many miles away from its home, from the forest it had always known, and brought it ashore on a strip of warm yellow sand, where it lay in the sun, quite still but breathing.

Vultures gathered and waited at a distance, some of them perching on the branches of nearby trees.

But the tiger was more drowned than hurt, and as the river water oozed out of his mouth, and the warm sun made new life throb through his body, he stirred and stretched, and his glazed eyes came into focus. Raising his head, he saw trees and tall grass.

Slowly he heaved himself off the ground and moved at a crouch to where the grass waved in the afternoon breeze. Would he be harried again, and shot at? There was no smell of Man. The tiger moved forward with greater confidence.

There was, however, another smell in the air—a smell that reached back to the time when he was young and fresh and full of vigour—a smell that he had almost forgotten but could never quite forget—the smell of a tigress!

He raised his head high, and new life surged through his tired limbs. He gave a full-throated roar and moved purposefully through the tall grass. And the roar came back to him, calling him, calling him forward—a roar that meant there would be more tigers in the land.